THE CLERK

GUILLERMO SACCOMANNO

OPEN LETTER
LITERARY TRANSLATIONS FROM THE UNIVERSITY OF ROCHE...

Library of Congress Cataloging-in-Publication Data: Available.
ISBN-13: 978-1-948830-25-6 / ISBN-10: 1-948830-25-6

*This project is supported in part by an award from the National Endowment for the Arts
and the New York State Council on the Arts with the support of Governor
Andrew M. Cuomo and the New York State Legislature.*

Printed on acid-free paper in the United States of America.

Cover Design by Alban Fischer
Interior Design by Anthony Blake

Open Letter is the University of Rochester's nonprofit, literary translation press:
Dewey Hall 1-219, Box 278968, Rochester, NY 14627

www.openletterbooks.org

PRAISE FOR GUILLERMO SACCOMANNO

"A choral, savage, and ruthless work, considered to be the great Argentine social novel." —*Europa Press*

"Like *Twin Peaks* reimagined by Roberto Bolaño, *Gesell Dome* is a teeming microcosm in which voices combine into a rich, engrossing symphony of human depravity." —*Publishers Weekly*

"Cynical and funny: a yarn worthy of a place alongside Cortázar and Donoso." —*Kirkus Reviews*

"By using a narrator who is not shocked, who does not look away from anything, Saccomanno shines a gruesome, graphic light on what people are willing to ignore so that their comfort remains intact." —Kim Fay, *Los Angeles Review of Books*

"*77* is a taut historical thriller with noir overtones. . . . As his characters grapple with love, allegiance, and daily life under a dictatorship, every action is a form of resistance." —*Foreword Reviews*

"*77* sings a dark song of one man's struggle to stay human when the inhumane lurks on every corner and the day-to-day reality of his world is curdled by the struggle between unchecked power and subversive acts." —Ross Nervig, *Southwest Review*

"A great novel. . . . I am—as we all should be—grateful for *77* and all novels like it." —Patrick Nathan, *Full Stop*

"*77* is ostensibly a novel about Argentina's Dirty War; it is also a book about reconciling inaction with survival." —*World Literature Today*

ALSO BY GUILLERMO SACCOMANNO

77

Gesell Dome

THE CLERK

To Ornella, together

. . . so extreme an experience of solitude
that one can only call it Russian.

FRANZ KAFKA, *The Diaries*

AT THIS TIME OF NIGHT, the armored helicopters fly over the
city, the bats flutter against the office windows, and the rats scurry
among the desks engulfed in darkness, all the desks but one, his,
with the computer turned on, the only one that's on at this hour.
The clerk feels a swift brushing against his shoes, a faint, fleeting
squeak that continues on its way along the carpet and slips away
into the blackness. He moves his eyes from the computer screen.
He sees the winged shadows in the night outside. Then he checks
his pocket watch, stacks some files, places the checks that the boss
will need to sign tomorrow in a folder, and gets up to leave. The
slowness of his movements isn't due only to fatigue. Also to sadness.

The computer takes a while to flicker off. At last the screen
grows dark, sighs. Carefully he arranges his office supplies for the
following day: pens, inkwell, stamps, stamp pad, eraser, pencil
sharpener, and letter opener. He gives the letter opener preferential
treatment. He polishes it. The letter opener looks harmless. But it
could end up being a weapon. He looks harmless, too. Appearances
can be deceiving, he says to himself.

[3]

He likes to think that, despite his meek character, under the right circumstances he might be fierce. If the proper circumstance presented itself, he could be someone else. Nobody is what they seem to be, he thinks. It's merely a matter of the right opportunity coming along and allowing him to reveal what he's capable of. This line of reasoning helps him put up with the boss, his coworkers, and his own family. No one knows who he is—not at the office and not at home. And if he considers that he doesn't know himself either, it makes him feel dizzy. One of these days they'll see. When they least expect it. It frightens him to dwell on the fact that, just as his boss, his coworkers, and his family don't know what he might be capable of, he doesn't know either. Sometimes when he's copying the boss's signature—and he copies it to perfection—he wonders who he is. He copies the boss's signature, secretly. Just because one person can copy another doesn't guarantee that he is the Other. More than once he's asked himself who he is, who he can become, if he can become someone else, but it scares him to find out. More than once he's thought about forging the boss's signature on a check, cashing it, and running away. If he hasn't done it yet, he reasons, it's because he has no one to share the spoils with. An extraordinary deed should be motivated by passion. In movies the hero always has a motive: a woman. If he were crazy in love with a woman, he wouldn't hesitate.

He puts away his office supplies, each one in its place. He arranges them with fanatical precision. And every so often he looks behind him. He looks at the desk behind his, where his closest coworker sits. Although that man isn't his subordinate, he does have tasks demanding fewer responsibilities, and one day, when the clerk is no longer there, he'll surely be the one to occupy his desk.

On more than one occasion the clerk has caught him writing in a notebook. When the other man noticed he was being observed, he stashed the notebook in one of his desk drawers, flashing an obsequious, embarrassed smile. At last the clerk confronted him. What are you writing, he asked. Frightened, the colleague replied that it was a diary, that he kept a diary, a personal one. The clerk didn't know what to say. Keeping a diary is a woman's thing, he thought. Maybe his coworker was gay. He didn't look it, but he might be. With other people, you can't tell. Keeping a diary sounds very interesting, he stammered. It had never occurred to him that the life of someone who spends his entire existence at a desk could be interesting. But he didn't say this out loud. One night like this, alone in the office, he rummaged through the drawers of the desk behind his. The notebook wasn't there. Then he imagined that there must be something directed against him in those pages. It was quite possible that his coworker had been assigned to track his movements. If that were true, he said to himself, even though he had always thought of himself as a helpful colleague and an ordinary citizen, he now found himself under surveillance. After a while he calmed down: if his coworker had been an agent and he a suspect, it wouldn't have been too long before he disappeared. Now their roles had been reversed. He'd gone from being observed to being the observer. His swift turn and the other man's haste in closing the notebook with that apologetic little smile was becoming a game that would eventually bore him. Since then he'd been convinced that his colleague, if he could, employing that same little smile, would take advantage of the tiniest error on his part just to move up one desk. Around here nobody can trust his own shadow. And the coworker behind him, he thinks, is his shadow. A threatening shadow, even if he *does* flash a friendly grin and is always ready to work on any file the clerk happens to toss his way.

The clerk focuses on the letter opener. If he plunged it into his colleague's jugular, it would be lethal. He upbraids himself for these sorts of fantasies. They debase him, he realizes. They make him feel vile. As vile as the others. Because deep down, he's convinced that he's better than the others. If the right opportunity came along, he could prove that he's above the rest and that his superiority, to put it bluntly, consists of not pulling the rug out from under someone else's feet just to garner a raise, a promotion. If he considers himself better than everybody else it's precisely because in the years he's been here, he's never tried to make himself stand out at the cost of harming the next guy. Not only that, he says to himself, but his behavior could be considered a stubborn desire to go unnoticed. Deep down, he reflects, if, in spite of his seniority in his position, he's never been the object of punitive action and still remains at his desk, it's because of his way of fitting in, which has ensured that no one takes too much notice of him. Sometimes he wonders whether, in order to have his colleagues think him harmless, he hasn't had to convince himself of the same thing first. When he reaches this point in his ruminations, he grows bitter. There's still the possibility that, after exerting so much effort to make himself appear like a man incapable of killing a fly, he's really become that man. But, at the same time, he thinks that anyone like him, with the talent to think of two contradictory ideas simultaneously, is not just superior to the rest but also a person to be feared, someone who, when least expected, can commit an act of rage that will leave the others to confront their own cowardice. Watch out, he says to himself. Watch out for me. Because I'm someone else. The fact that I don't show it now doesn't mean that, if an opportunity arises, others have the right to put me down. And among the others, the one who should be the most careful, of course, is my coworker.

When he's finished straightening up his desk, he walks over to the coat rack, takes down his overcoat. It embarrasses him to wear this overcoat, which, besides being threadbare, has lost its shape over the years. But as cold as it's been these past few weeks, with the temperature dropping more every day, he has no choice but to wear it. Every morning, before entering the building, he takes it off, folds it, and keeps it folded over his arm, revealing the new lining he had put in last year at the Bolivian tailor shop in his neighborhood. At the office, looking to both sides, he stealthily hangs it up on a distant coat rack, in a corner, way in back. And he walks away immediately.

In his haste he fears that someone may notice his uneven gait. In general, he manages to minimize his limp with a measured way of walking. But when he leaves his overcoat on the coat rack, it's hard for him not to rush off, as if the overcoat belonged to someone else. However, at this time of night, alone in the office, he takes down the overcoat and slips into it calmly. He turns off the lamp and, shrouded in darkness, decides to leave. He can walk blindly between the desks: so great is his familiarity, his instinctive memory of the place, the cabinets, the nooks, and odd corners.

But certain sounds stop him in his tracks. It's not the rats. It's footsteps.

2

ON THE FROSTED GLASS DOOR OF THE BOSS'S OFFICE, a shadow
is projected. He sees it slide along the glass, outlined by helicopter
searchlights. No one else stays so late at the office. No one but him
puts in so much overtime. He does so not just out of necessity, but
by choice. He wants to delay going home for as long as possible.
But tonight, fear makes him regret having stayed. He lies in wait
for the shadow behind the frosted glass, letter opener in hand, fear
coursing through his body.

He listens closely. Footsteps on the other side. If those footsteps
belong to a thief, and if he, with his clumsy heroism, manages to
subdue that thief, the boss will reward his action and possibly even
obliterate the debts he's contracted from advances on his salary. He
tiptoes by, trying to keep his limp from giving him away, to keep the
leather of his worn-out shoes from squeaking. He crouches to one
side of the door.

The footsteps on the other side cease. The silence expands. He
fears he'll lose his nerve. His whole life has been marked by submission; this might be his great opportunity. If he blows it, he may
never get another one. And the memory of this night, he knows,
would become yet another frustration, the umpteenth in his life.

He'll wait until the intruder comes out of the office; he'll throw
himself on him, grab him by the neck, and with the letter opener at
his throat, he'll disarm him, because the intruder will certainly have
a weapon, a firearm. He'll take control of the weapon, and pointing
it at the other man, he'll call for the building security guards.

As the door opens, the shadow on the floor expands.

3

HE PREPARES TO LAUNCH THE ATTACK. But he holds back. The secretary is terrified when she sees him crouching, about to stab her with the letter opener. Her eyeglasses fall off. He can hardly speak. He picks up the young woman's glasses, round ones. He stammers an explanation, still clutching the letter opener. The young woman trembles. He leaves the letter opener on the desk. The helicopter searchlights pass across the windows. He can see the shimmer of her tears. Trying to calm her, he wraps her in an embrace.

The faces and their lips, their bodies: fused. The clerk steps back with exaggerated gallantry. He'll have to remember this moment forever, he tells himself. For the first time he feels that his cowardice isn't as great as he's grown accustomed to believing, and that deep down, as he thought a while ago, he's capable of inconceivable acts. As he soothes the young woman, while she puts her glasses back on, he turns on a lamp and offers her a glass of water. He's regained his nerve now. But he notices that he's wearing his overcoat. He's about to take it off. He hesitates. But he leaves it on. In the half-darkness, the deplorable state of the coat isn't so obvious. He walks over to the mineral water dispenser. He returns with a plastic cup.

She thanks him. The mere word *thanks* fills him with a sensation he's never experienced before. He watches her take a drink. Her nervous sips delight him. In the silence of the room, beyond the lamplight, the bats' screeches become birdsong. She says she's feeling better. But her gaze is erratic. He's reassured by the fact that she hasn't noticed his overcoat. He offers to walk her home, with her permission. At this time of night, the subway is dangerous and the buses go by sporadically. At this hour—almost midnight—it would be unwise for her to walk alone through the deserted streets. The only ones roaming about at this hour are gang members, the homeless, and cloned dogs. He'll feel more at ease if he walks her back, he says. She blinks, sighs. With a doll-like smile, she accepts. She looks younger in those round glasses. He sees his reflection in the young woman's lenses, doubly reflected in two small, circular mirrors that reproduce him in miniature.

They leave the office, walk down the deserted corridor, and their footsteps on the tiled floor echo throughout the building. The clerk rings for the elevator. The gears and their gloomy reverberation. They ride down silently. She stares at the floor. He watches the numbers flickering on the control panel. He looks at the secretary out of the corner of his eye: the round glasses, the upturned nose, the chestnut-colored hair in a boy cut, the tailored suit buttoned up like a uniform. They could keep on descending to the ends of the earth and he'd feel just as happy. Beside her, nothing else matters to him. He'd love to open up, surrender to her. If only she would love him, he would gladly ride straight down to hell. Because hell is the sub-basement of the self, he thinks. A basement where no one can lie to others or to himself. This is the worst punishment that can be inflicted on someone: to take away all their illusions of vanity, even the tiniest one. Suddenly he fears that, besides his limp, she'll discover other defects in him, those that are least visible.

As they emerge into the street, the evening fog obstructs their view of the helicopters circling above them. The engines, that rumbling of the propellers, are quite a presence: dark steel insects with yellow, expectant eyes. A searchlight drills through the fog, illuminates them, and vanishes again. The empty downtown streets, streets with banks, architectural fortresses. Every so often they come across bodies sleeping among cardboard boxes, curled up in arcades and entryways. The clerk and the secretary step around the sprawled bodies. They turn onto a pedestrian street. Here, too, they encounter men, women, and children sleeping all bundled up between the shops' display windows. The couple holds their breath at the stench of those bodies. They turn aside to avoid some zombie kids. One of them walks toward them, slobbering; the clerk takes the secretary's arm, and preemptively changes sides with her. The kid trips, hesitates, mutters hoarsely, and continues on his way, in a trance. Protecting the young woman gives the clerk a confidence that distinguishes him from the mouse he was a while ago, hunched over the files, as the helicopters focused their lights on the building, the bats fluttered by the office windows, and the rats scurried beneath the desks. Hardly more than an hour has gone by since then, he says to himself, checking his watch: it's after midnight. And yet it seems to him that the young woman's sudden appearance in his life happened so long ago. Back when he was someone else. And this person he now has become, on remembering the Other, has the impression that his other self was nothing but an ancestor. In Laos, he once read in a magazine, after an epidemic the sick change their names. Maybe he's become Laotian now. Love is a sickness that turns you Laotian, he says to himself. It makes you someone else.

However, in spite of the self-confidence inspired in him by escorting the young woman, he can't help wondering about hell. Which is the greater hell, he wonders: hell as a sub-basement of oneself, just as he imagined it a while ago, or this thing right in front of his nose, abject poverty, bodies curled up in a doorway, covered with newspaper and piss-stained blankets, guarding their only possessions in a bag or a supermarket cart. At least those who have fallen so low, he consoles himself, no longer have to stay up nights, anxiously, obsequiously, desperately hanging on to a desk; they're free of paranoia, machinations, and conspiratorial suspicions.

Choppy, their conversation. Nonetheless, he probes into the young woman's life. Cautiously he tries to avoid being overly curious and discreetly reacts to the occasional anecdote. He doesn't want to come across as a fool. Sometimes he interrupts with an expression of confusion. She talks about the boss. She talks about the boss too much. She takes care of his concerns all the time. He doesn't feel jealous of the boss, but it bothers him that she devotes so much of the conversation to him. Until she starts talking about their office mate. She talks about the office mate as much as about the boss.

Maybe she even expounds more on the office mate than on the boss. Which, he tells her, is strange. And this makes it interesting. He should measure the time she allots to each one in order to be sure of what he suspects. They walk toward the subway entrance. He looks at the young woman. And he wonders what could be wrong with this complicity between them that goes beyond the bounds of collegiality. Better not to overthink this feeling, what might lie beneath it, a mere glimpse of which fills him with fear.

It's cold. The young woman shivers. He does as well, though he tries to deny it; his teeth are chattering. At last he decides. At this time of night the subway is dangerous, he says to her. He takes off his overcoat and places it around the young woman's shoulders.

He hails a taxi.

4

THE TAXI IN THE NIGHT. An uncomfortable silence isolates them. If he lets the silence take over, she'll withdraw. So he tells a joke. She smiles. She covers the smile with her hands. The young woman's shy reaction, an inhibition when she separates her lips, conceals a missing bicuspid. Her modesty moves him. He's about to tell her another joke, but he holds back. He wants to appear understanding, not clownish. During a sharp turn, the young woman is thrown against him. He stops her. Then he helps her back into the seat.

When the taxi comes to the edge of a park, some cloned dogs cross in front of it. Frantic barking. A plague, those dogs. The taxi charges into them. It tosses one of them into the air, where it remains suspended for a few seconds above the engine. The driver, unfazed, doesn't blink an eye. He rolls down the window and spits into the night.

They travel practically stuck together. The secretary was shocked by the dog attack, the taxi running them over. If she lived in a bigger apartment, she says, she'd love to have a pet. But not a cloned one. Cloned pets don't have the same feelings as real ones, she explains.

A call on her cell phone interrupts her. Annoyed, she turns it off. We're almost there, she says. The next highway exit. He remains silent. That phone call, he thinks. That call in the night. She seems to guess what he's thinking. No, she has no boyfriend, she tells him. And she asks if he's a jealous type. Not at all, he says. But he can't help thinking about that call. She's hiding something from him, he senses. If she's hiding it, he thinks, it must be because it's a secret relationship. It's quite possible that she's involved in a compromising romance. Maybe with someone from the office. If he keeps following that line of thought, he'll figure out who it is. Someone near her in at the office. And the one who's closest to her, after him, is the coworker behind him. It hadn't occurred to him till now: pleasant, affable, with that little smile, the coworker embodies all the qualities of a workplace suitor. Besides, the fact that he carries around a personal diary must be an infallible argument for passing himself off as a poet. That lowlife wants to seduce her just as sure as he's aiming to occupy his position. The only thing standing between the coworker's desk and the secretary's is his own desk. An excellent reason why the coworker is plotting to get him out of the way. Suddenly, the colleague, in addition to being his rival in the office, takes on the role of a dangerous opponent in the secretary's seduction. He needs to put a halt to this suspicion right now. It makes no sense, he says to himself. Besides, realistically, he must admit his own insignificance: he doesn't stand a chance of winning over the young woman. He's no seducer. He never was. And he doesn't see why he should be one now. Once again he rebels against these fantasies that look to him like the delirium of a man in love. He has enough problems in his life without romancing a secretary. Once more his imagination has turned against him. An unbridled imagination, he thinks, is the illness of those who spend too much time locked up indoors. And this is the case with him. He really should put in less overtime.

The journey ends in a run-down neighborhood on the outskirts of the city. A few apartment buildings rise between an empty lot and a slum. In this area there are few helicopters. The wire fence that separates the slum from the buildings is guarded by a patrol car. The cops snore. Not very far away, on the next block, at the base of a building, there's a kiosk and some drunken kids. A gust of wind carries a cumbia melody and laughter from the kiosk. The wind sweeps the area. The stench of toxic waste from factories and laboratories. Also in the air is the sweet-and-sour density emanating from the rural settlements.

Like other secretaries, the young woman no doubt assumes that, by having risen to a position connected with the company hierarchy, she occupies a higher social rank. With her glamorous appearance, she doesn't seem like a salaried worker, but rather a modern young woman with a favorable future. If her office mates knew that she lives in a slum, she would die of shame. It touches him to think that she might feel ashamed.

The taxi stops at the last apartment block. He pays without asking the driver to wait. As he pays for the ride, he worries that she might notice that he has just enough money and that he'll go home by subway. He walks her to the entrance. The farewell moment. She notices his sadness. She invites him up to her apartment for a cup of coffee. He can't refuse, he says.

He can hardly contain his happiness.

5

INSIDE THE BUILDING, the heat intensifies the combined odor of floral-scented room deodorizer and cooking oil. In the stillness a baby is crying. They walk toward the elevator. The scissor gate opens and closes with a dull thud. They ride up in silence. They get out. They walk some more. Their footsteps, the echoes of their steps on the tiles, the jingling of the young woman's keys. They're the only two living beings in this tomb.

She rents a two-room apartment. He's captivated by the décor: painted plates on the walls, small porcelain figurines, doilies and tablecloths beneath vases with artificial flowers, a profusion of teddy bears piled on a chair, an Oriental-style rug. On a dresser, family photos. The young woman points out her parents, her brothers and sisters, a sister-in-law, and also a little nephew, whom she adores.

The clerk observes the photo of her parents and then observes her, looking for common traits. They died, she says. The nursing home caught fire, she says. The clerk doesn't know what to say. It's outrageous, he declares, there are more and more fires in nursing homes all the time. His anger is exaggerated. Just like killer kids in schools, she adds. Two weeks ago one of them walked into the classroom with a machine gun and wiped out his whole class. Then he did the same thing to another class. And another. He kept going till he ran out of ammunition. Then he blew himself up with a hand grenade. She looks sad as she tells the story. The family, he says. The family is responsible, he says. Always the family. Because home is the first school. He says it in a sententious tone. She agrees.

Now he looks at two framed diplomas, one in Accounting and the other for teaching English. On another wall is a picture of the young woman, as a girl, in her white First Communion dress. Immaculate, with a rosary and a mother-of-pearl catechism between her prayerfully folded hands, she looks like the secretary's little sister.

She withdraws to the kitchen to make coffee. But the phone rings. And she picks up ahead of the answering machine. She turns the volume all the way down. Annoyed, she looks at the device. She hates people who don't respect others' privacy after a certain hour, she says.

Who is she referring to when she says "people," he wonders. Saying "people" is the same as saying "nobody." A lover, he thinks. That call in the taxi must have been a lover, too. The same lover who called her earlier. And who else could it be but his office mate. Maybe, fearful that the affair might be revealed, she decided to end it, and now the jilted colleague can't accept it, won't give up, and insists on keeping it going. Left alone, the clerk is overcome by uncertainty. He goes back to look at the communion photo. And suddenly he wonders what he's doing in this apartment at this time of night. He can't help it: the communion photo weakens his resolve. Then his eyes linger on a little silver bell for calling servants. He picks it up carefully. If the secretary were his employer and he her servant, he imagines, as soon as he heard the little bell he'd come running to satisfy her every whim. Delicately, to prevent the bell from ringing, he deposits it back where it was: between two terracotta elephants.

Tomorrow—and tomorrow will be very soon—when he wakes up, he'll believe that this night was a dream. The only way to convince himself that the dream was real would be to help himself to a souvenir. He's about to take a tiny, pink crystal swan. But he doesn't do it. By merely sliding his finger along these objects, he realizes that there's not a single speck of dust. It seems that the young woman treasures these pieces like a personal museum. It frightens him to think that when she goes back and inspects her knickknack collection, she might notice an absence and suspect him.

[17]

It's important that he appreciate every moment. Because later, even tomorrow, when he remembers this night, he'll try to reconstruct it. He'll rhapsodize over the little porcelain cups that the secretary now carries on a wicker tray and respect the fact that the little coffee cups and the tray, even if they *were* bought on clearance at a street fair, reflect a concern for beauty in their decorative earnestness. From a shiny wooden chest with glass doors, she removes two cut-crystal glasses and a bottle of brandy. He shouldn't drink alcohol, he tells himself. But he can't refuse. He savors the brandy.

What would it be like to kiss her, he wonders.

6

A SHIPWRECK, SHE SAYS. He heard her: she's a refugee from a shipwreck. It's enough for her to say shipwreck. A real romantic opportunity, he thinks. If he were involved in a shipwreck, aboard a boat with room enough for only two passengers, and if he, the oarsman, had to deal with the dilemma of choosing the survivors, he would choose the young woman without hesitation, and, if necessary, he'd beat the other shipwreck victims on their heads and faces with his oar. He doesn't want to imagine what he'd do if, instead of an oar, he had an axe. He wouldn't hesitate to split skulls, lop off fingers and arms, and save only her.

The young woman explains that her shipwreck was an emotional one. She's trying to stay afloat. He knows what she's talking about. He's capsizing too, he thinks. Or rather, it's been a long time since he capsized. If only she knew, he thinks. But he doesn't have the nerve to tell her his history. They're two castaways. She, with her embarrassment over her missing bicuspid, and he with his overcoat. Two embarrassments that find one another. The coincidence proves that their destinies were fated to meet. It was written. But where was it written, he asks himself. In heaven, he thinks, answering his own question. Imagine heaven as a vast department with infinite divisions in which the destinies of souls are classified and stored in file folders. Some celestial scribe detected an affinity between two files, the secretary's and his. The only thing you can hope for is that the classification isn't one of those typical bureaucratic mistakes, like those he could easily make at the office, an ordinary slip-up, which, for the person involved in the file, might be the beginning of an endless string of troubles.

He chides himself for these musings. He needs to work things out as quickly as possible to make the young woman understand that tonight has ignited him. He also needs to wait till she finishes the story of her romantic disillusionment, the shipwreck, as she calls it. A broken heart, the young woman says. Also: broken promises, withered hopes, short-lived reconciliations, useless dressings on a wound. She shakes with sobs. He finds her shudders charming, no less her bouts of hiccups, the spasms of a forlorn little girl. Even when she exaggerates with her flood of tears, snot, Kleenex, she suffers. He envies the guy who's making her suffer, who—he thinks once more—can't be anyone but his office mate. And with these thoughts, he feels like a fool: how could he not have realized that the guy, seen from a female perspective, could be considered attractive. Because women can find a despicable guy attractive. It must have been his office mate who called her twice this evening.

The clerk doesn't know what to feel: a sense of triumph as long as the young woman resists those phone calls, or anguish for the sadness that makes her shudder. Pained, he asks the secretary to tell him everything if that will give her some relief. To consider him a friend. There's nothing like a friend when loneliness drives you into a corner. She shouldn't consider him a colleague, he explains. He's a friend. She dries her tears. If he swears to keep the secret, she'll reveal who that man is. He says his lips are sealed.

The boss, she replies.

7

HE REMAINS SPEECHLESS, CALM, looking her in the eye. He thinks about the boss. The boss's greasy bald spot, the boss's bushy eyebrows, the boss's pock-marked nose, the boss's sour breath. Also: his impeccable shirts, his flashy ties, his prominent gut, and his pants with suspenders. And the ring. He can't forget about the ring: impressive, with a carving that looks like a seal. He also can't forget: the boss's shoes, black, highly polished, with rubber soles. The boss likes to skulk around silently, making his subordinates fear his sudden appearance.

He wonders how she could have become involved with that sort of guy. She was duped, he thinks. With the same slyness with which the boss wears his rubber-soled shoes, he must have set a trap for the young woman, pretending to be kind-hearted. The boss sweet-talked her in that half-paternal, half-fatuous style of those who know their own power. He must have hinted at a promotion.

He can't take his eyes off the answering machine. So it was the boss who called her twice tonight. Before, on her cell phone, when they were in the taxi. Now, at her house.

The décor, which until just now had struck him as typical of a taste sensitive to beauty, now seems vulgar and tacky. It wouldn't surprise him if it had been the boss who gave her those teddy bears. That big-bellied bear with a necktie, for example. He feels like an idiot. It's hard for him to listen to her. He wished he hadn't found out: the boss is married, but she didn't care because she thought the boss was a good man. This story wounds him. He ought to leave right now.

He wants to escape, disappear into the night once and for all. Once and for all. And forever. But he can't. With a heavy heart, he hands the young woman another Kleenex. They're so close again, both of them on the same sofa, he with one arm extended along the backrest. She tips her head back and leans on his arm. The young woman is wearing a subtle perfume. She doesn't want to think, she tells him. She's so confused. Then, at last, he works up the nerve to kiss her, and she, as if in a swoon, surrenders to the kiss, which is clumsy and hot. He doesn't close his eyes. She closes hers, but, as the kiss goes on and on, she opens them again, and both sets of eyes regard each other.

He checks his watch; he's ready to leave. In a quavering voice, she asks him not to go, she doesn't want to be alone, she's scared of being alone. But he shouldn't misunderstand. She has to face her loneliness. And loneliness has become terrifying. If he leaves now, she doesn't know what she'll do. Please stay. At least until she falls asleep.

He wonders what things will be like later, in the morning, when they meet at the office. He wonders how he'll face the boss. He also wonders how the young woman will act, if the boss will realize that an intimate relationship has developed between two of his subordinates. Better not to think, as she says. She takes his hand and leads him to her bedroom. On the nightstand are some lit candles, incense.

This can't be happening to him. It's too good. It's someone else she's leading to her bed. It'll be easier if he thinks it's someone else. Maybe he doesn't have to idealize the following scene: a man and a woman, discovering one another in the darkness, touching one another, peeling off their clothes and at the same time undressing one another, fingers freeing a button, lowering a zipper, a caress beneath their undergarments, a strap, a nipple, another zipper, the glans, some elastic, the clitoris. His hands are damp and cold. He apologizes. It's nerves, she whispers. Her hands are cold, too. And her feet. Her feet are freezing. It's circulation, she explains. Her feet are always freezing.

He assumes that he, a hot-blooded man, should take the initiative and not, as things are developing, let her be his guide. If she, despite her youth, is making the rules, it's because she has experience. She's not as innocent as he imagined. Again he was naïve. Her fleshy mouth, her sharp teeth that nibble him, the sensuality she infects him with, all make him reconsider: the times she must have repeated these maneuvers with others. He'll screw up if he doesn't stop thinking. Maybe his assumptions about the young woman come from his own fear of not functioning. It's quite possible that the young woman's urgency is the result of deferred needs. Of passion.

The virus. Remembering the virus paralyzes him. Millions of victims all over the planet. As he thinks about the virus, he goes flaccid. And yet, if he mentions the risk of the virus he'll seem like a gentleman. With the young woman mounting him, panting, he manages to ask her if she has condoms. If he's worried, she replies, the condoms are in the nightstand. He's no Don Juan, he explains. If he were, he'd go around with a supply of condoms all the time. He shouldn't make such a production of it, she says. She wants to feel him. He reasons that if she has condoms in the nightstand, so close at hand, it's because she must have used them with the boss. To avoid pregnancy, he thinks. Although there's also another possibility: that she uses them to protect herself from the boss's promiscuity. No doubt this young woman isn't the only one the boss is screwing. But, if he considers the young woman's actions tonight, why not think that, in addition to the boss, she has other lovers. He realizes that if he goes on with these conjectures, he'll ruin the night.

He wouldn't mind dying between her legs.

8

DAYBREAK. The clerk ventures into the early morning mist. His limping footsteps. He raises the lapels of his overcoat. The shadow of a streetlamp, puddles. It's too late. Or too early. At this hour of the morning, the subway trains run infrequently. He needs to get back home as soon as possible.

He often remarks to his friends that his home and family are very precious to him in these times of moral crisis. He's referring to his wife and kids, his loved ones, beneficiaries of a good education, grounded in sacrifice and affection. He takes pleasure in talking about home and family. The family atmosphere he describes at the office bears no resemblance to the truth. The home is a rented apartment near a terminal on the outskirts of the city, a three-room place facing the back of the building: dark, close, and fetid. His wife, a lump with horsey features, is a sour, despotic sort, and his children a litter of obese, ill-behaved brats.

They demand electronic devices, fashionable clothing, astronaut-style sneakers, a car, vacations. Those ingrates should be glad his salary stretches far enough to let them go to bed with their bellies stuffed full of hamburgers, sausages, fries, and sodas. Sometimes he has trouble telling them apart. All of them look so much like their mother. More like her every day. Sometimes he imagines himself murdering them.

All of them except El Viejito, "the little old man," the only one who's different from that screeching mass, that pale, albino child with one white eye, his faced crossed by little blue veins, wizened, his skeleton looking as if it were made of wire instead of bones. Always hunched over, looking up from underneath, this child of his, the sickliest one. With his extreme shyness, El Viejito always goes around silently, protecting himself from a spanking that might rain down upon him. The clerk isn't unaware of the fact that out of the entire litter, this puny child is the one who most resembles him. Like his father, El Viejito has a limp.

In a travel and popular science magazine, he reads an article about the discovery of a sixteen-million-year-old, pre-human skull in the south. It's estimated that the skull belongs to a subspecies of monkey the size of a cat, but with a large head, surprisingly large, a fact that, according to the magazine, suggests the extraordinary size of its brain. Living in trees prevented this little monkey from walking erect. The clerk cannot look at El Viejito without thinking of that monkey. El Viejito is also the exception who, unlike his littermates, inspires feelings of something other than revulsion: he pities El Viejito. More than a son of his, El Viejito is a cellmate. Every time he thinks about El Viejito, he feels an impotent rage. He would have liked for one of his children, just one, to be different. Not a superman, the thinks, but at least someone normal. Which isn't too much to ask. Maybe there's something wrong with his blood. And that something makes it inferior. El Viejito is the example.

If he calls him El Viejito, it's because there is no other description that better suits the poor kid. It pains him not to think about El Viejito all the time. But you can't think about the victims all the time if you want to keep living, he says to himself.

9

BARKING IN THE DISTANCE. Cloned dogs. Deserted streets and avenues. He runs toward the subway. The barking comes closer. He hates to run. Because of his limp. The subway entrance. The dogs in pursuit. The barking descends the stairs. Luckily a train is coming. The doors open. And they close before the pack of dogs can get on.

It's a forty-minute trip to his house. Frozen, in one of the last seats, he rubs his hands together for warmth. When he gets home, he'll need a plausible excuse to explain why he's returning from the office at this hour. He can invent an alibi: that he was stopped by a police raid. He sniffs his fingers: the young woman's odor. His whole body must smell of her. As soon as he gets home, he'll lock himself in the bathroom. He hopes his wife won't catch him showering at this time of the morning.

The subway train slows down. As he gets off, he rehearses what he'll say. He walks along, talking to himself. When he reaches the building, he's paralyzed. His mouth is dry. Before he walks in, he hears a distant explosion. He can see flames rising at the end of the street. Another attack.

The elevator isn't working. He takes the stairs. Before entering his apartment, he waits for his breathing to return to normal. He enters in the dark. Like a child who, after a misdeed, shrinks before the inevitable punishment. The warm darkness smells of fried food, tobacco, dirty clothes, and, in an attempt to mask that dense stink, of eucalyptus boiling in an aluminum pitcher on top of a heater. He wishes he could keep the secretary's perfume clinging to his whole body. But he needs to be careful. He imagines the furious woman leading the litter of fatties, all of them advancing between the desks, toward the young woman. He hurriedly showers. He puts his clothes back on. Enveloped in the steam, he opens the little window and waits for the bathroom to air out.

He wipes the clouded mirror with a towel. Dejected, he looks at his reflection. Pallor, glassy eyes. He begins to shave. And cuts himself. On the neck. A few drops of blood fall into the sink. Facing the mirror, he watches himself bleed. The drops of blood in the sink are a message. If only he were capable of murdering the family, he thinks. The blood goads him on. After all, what do they expect from life. A car, appliances, designer sneakers, video games, surround sound, giant TVs. Destiny can't be an automatic dishwasher or a pair of jeans. He'll buy poison, a mechanical saw, and . . . show time! But the plan presents several obstacles, from which poison to choose and where to buy it, to the butchery skills needed to cut up the bodies, the stringent cleanliness of the kitchen, the whole apartment, of carrying out the remains in plastic bags, spreading them around, which means evading military checkpoints. He can't imagine himself going back and forth with bags full of body parts. Parks, garbage dumps, construction sites, the port. He would need to figure out an explanation for his family's mysterious disappearance. Less problematic, he reflects, would be a gas leak. That kind of death would be less painful for all of them, and, besides, easy to explain. He arrives home from the office, smells the gas, verifies that everyone is dead, and, in the end, after opening the windows, he calls for an ambulance, the police. With either of these two options, poison or gas, to leave El Viejito alive would be an issue. He's sorry to have to include El Viejito.

It takes a while for the steam in the bathroom to evaporate. His cut won't stop bleeding. He could stand there his whole life long, watching himself bleed, the drops falling, exploding in the sink. There's less steam now.

The woman is in the doorway, watching him.

THE WOMAN, A CIGARETTE DANGLING FROM HER MOUTH, asks him what he's doing.

It's unlikely she suspects adultery, he thinks.

What are you doing, she insists.

I couldn't sleep, he replies. Insomnia, he explains.

With a serious expression, the woman looks at the blood in the sink. She sticks a finger in the blood and sucks it. She X-rays him: if he's stringing together a pack of lies, he ought to be careful. The woman is enormous, and the bathroom, minuscule. She shoves him aside so she can sit on the toilet. She blows cigarette smoke in his face. If he's planning to do himself in, she says, before he splits for the Great Beyond he should settle his debts in the Great Here and Now. He doesn't respond. When she gets riled up, she ends up hitting him. This wouldn't be the first time she gives him a good beating. Nor the last. On more than one occasion he's kneeled before her, begging her to calm down, pleading that this scene is a degrading lesson for the children, and a real spectacle for the neighbors. But the kids celebrate the beatings. The only one who trembles, who runs and hides when she hits him is El Viejito. After each beating, when he returns to the office and his colleagues point out a bruise, he blushes and invents some accident.

A towel, swiped quickly across his face. He escapes. There's a couch in the living room. There's still a little time before he has to go to work. He needs to sleep. He tries to remember the last time he slept beside his wife in their marriage bed. He wonders what became of that young woman he met years ago, possessed of a slenderness that, in those days, impressed him as charmingly fragile. He remembers. He remembers that he dreamed of sleeping with his arms around the young woman's tiny breasts. But one morning, when he opened his eyes, there was that thing, snoring beside him. Overcome with revulsion, he moved to the sofa.

It's not the difference between what we were and what we are that brings us down, he thinks. It's the laziness with which we give in to degradation.

11

HE'S CURLED UP ON THE COUCH, SLEEPING, but he's jolted awake by the flushing of the water tank, the bathroom door, and the woman, who approaches him, snorting with rage. In a fetal position, his eyes squeezed shut, he hides deep inside himself. The woman, in shadows, covers him with his overcoat. You'd better not catch the flu and have to stay home from work. All we need is for you to lose your job, she mutters. If they throw you out on the street, I'll break every bone in your body.

Through the window that faces the street, the sound of traffic now grows more intense. The darkness persists while the city gears up. He has to fall asleep quickly, before the morning lights up the humidity-stained walls and the apartment starts buzzing with activity. He doggedly tries to sleep, but can't. His eyes hurt. He needs rest. His back feels stiff. Once again his eyelids squeeze shut, trying to sleep. Dawn overtakes him. A grayish clarity outlines the room. The dark furniture against the dull green walls. Then the secretary comes to his rescue. She arrives wrapped in an ethereal light. A breeze ruffles her hair like in a shampoo commercial. She smiles radiantly. Her bicuspid is no longer missing.

The alarm clock vibrates throughout the apartment.

MORNING AT LAST. Through the window rises the clamor of military trucks, the honking of horns, buses, sirens, cars. The scrape of a match lighting a burner. A teapot coming to a boil. The noise of the toaster. A yawn. A throat being cleared. A faucet. Slippers. The voices of the litter emerging from its lethargy. Then: shouts, arguments, insults, wailing. He can't distinguish the cough of one of them from the head cold of another. Amid the stagnation that spreads through the dwelling, it's hard for him to remember exactly how many the litter consists of, what their names are. They all inherited his traits. But, as they grew fatter, these traits became caricatures. He can barely identify them or even tell the boys and girls apart. It's true that all of them—male and female—resemble him in some ways, but that evil expression they bear isn't his. Maternal line, people say. El Viejito, on the other hand, lacks that treacherous air. Maybe El Viejito isn't really so good. Maybe El Viejito just pretends to be the good one, which isn't the same thing, and exploits his victimhood. Not one of them, neither boys nor girls, resembles him as much as El Viejito, who now peeks furtively through a doorway. This son of his, with his white eye and his inherited limp.

The woman can't start her day without the news. As soon as she gets up, before washing her face and making coffee, she lights a cigarette and turns on the TV with the volume all the way up. This morning a guerrilla commando took credit for blowing up a private neighborhood in the hills surrounding the city. The number of victims has not yet been determined. An oil field was the target of another attack. Losses in the millions. Dozens of terrorists were brought down in conflicts with the army. Their relatives and friends were arrested. As investigations of its organization move ahead, the government has declared that it will not seek a truce despite threats. The populace is warned that peaceful demonstrations will be considered aiding and abetting terrorists and will therefore be suppressed with the full power of the law. The subway will operate during regular hours today. An impersonal newscaster reports the number of deaths this month due to terrorism, attacks, robberies, rapes, plane accidents, auto accidents, traffic accidents, and accidents in the workplace. At daybreak, in a slum, reports of a shootout between Peruvian and Colombian drug traffickers. Late-breaking news: There has been an attack at a clinic that was experimenting with cloning babies.

The woman doesn't remain in front of the screen. She runs through the house, screaming at the litter, distributing smacks to their heads and using the TV like a radio. She's not worried about the attacks or the massacres. Only domestic crimes. In a fit of jealousy, a woman castrates her husband. A man knifes his mistress's silicone breasts. A mother seasons her children's formula with rat poison. A grandson roasts his grandparents in the oven. If the domestic violence is especially lurid, she runs to the TV and stands there, mesmerized. These types of crimes attract her, crimes as ordinary as a family recipe. If the news generates a debate, she always takes the side of the accused and argues with the emcee, the panelists, and the interviewees. Only she, as defense attorney, seems to understand the motives of the accused. When she diverts her gaze from the TV to her husband, he senses what's going through her head and wonders how long it will be before she gets the notion to switch from spectator to protagonist.

Next, the weather report. Due to global warming, the storm front sweeping over the city will continue. Expect strong winds and acid rain.

He wants to go into the kitchen. But he's run over by the litter. The kitchen is the corral where fights break out. Anything is enough to provoke a battle. A smidgen of cold cuts, a spoonful of *dulce de leche*, a slice of toast.

The woman lashes out at the litter. A nose starts to bleed. A tooth breaks. A black eye. The woman imposes order with her fists. They leave her alone.

He pours himself some coffee. Less and less time till he leaves for the office. He wonders what the young woman would think if she saw him under these conditions.

THE COFFEE CEASEFIRE DOESN'T LAST LONG. They grab him by
the shirt. A fat little girl in braids. She asks him for some coins. He
wants to get rid of this little mooch. But he can't: she's his daughter.
To get rid of her, he looks for coins in his pocket. He hands her
one. The little girl looks at the coin. She's not satisfied with just
one. She kicks his ankle. He steps back. The girl kicks him again.
Why doesn't he grab her by the hair, he asks himself, and throw
her out the window that faces the airshaft. In the uproar of screams
and slaps emanating from the other side of the apartment, nobody
would hear the greedy little pig fall. He leans over toward the girl.
He tries to convince her that it's not nice for a little girl to attack her
daddy. He strokes her hair. The girl scratches him. Then the woman
comes over and drags her away by a braid.

From another corner of the kitchen, he hears the woman, like
a general, ordering the litter to count off. She lines them up and
sends them off to school. The sound of asthmatic wheezing under
the table attracts his attention. El Viejito crawls toward him and
embraces his legs. He doesn't want to go along with the litter. He
cries, calling him Daddy. His white eye cries, too. The clerk feels a
lump in his throat. The woman returns for the boy; she traps him.
El Viejito clutches his father's pants. The woman grabs El Viejito
by the back of the neck. She takes him over to the others. From
the living room comes the laughter of the rest of the pack. Then, a
smack and the bang of a door slamming.

Why hasn't one of those murderous kids come to his kids'
school yet, the kind that one fine day blasts his classmates with
gunfire, he wonders. Today might be the lucky day, he thinks hope-
fully. Though it wouldn't be so great if the gunshots also eliminated
El Viejito.

Still in the kitchen, he barely moves. He emerges from his corner. He removes one cracker from a tin, and just as he's about to put

it in his mouth, the woman challenges him. Those are *her* crackers, she says. He returns the cracker to the tin. Why is he still hanging around, she asks. Maybe he doesn't feel like going to work, she assaults him. She can't stand him anymore; she's fed up. She's wasted the best years of her life with him, she says. The best years, she repeats. He ruined her future, a future that's gone now. The woman takes away the tin of crackers and stores it in the cupboard. And to think she could have married that military man, she complains. He lowers his head. She can't tolerate his cowardice, she says. She spits as she talks to him. She shakes him: she orders him to look at what's become of her, all because of him. She wasn't like this before. She was young, pretty; she had boyfriends and she was sexy. How sexy she was before she married him. Generous, too, she reminds him. She was good-natured.

He knows that her tantrum is endangering his physical wellbeing. As soon as she turns around to stash the tin of crackers in the pantry, he escapes. He really should change his shirt, his tie. But it's better not to expose himself. He picks up his overcoat from the sofa and leaves, tripping over everything in his way: some toys, a chair, the TV, which is disconnected when his foot gets stuck in the cable. Once out in the hallway, he doesn't even stop to wait for the elevator. He leaps down the stairs, reaches the street.

14

THE DIN OF THE CITY, the endless stream of cars and buses that start and stop, get stuck and lurch forward, one after another, united as in a convoy. The nervous throng that overflows the sidewalks, waiting for buses, or rushing into the subway entrance. Man is a creature of habit, he says to himself as he breathes the polluted street air, the impenetrable fog of fuel. But unlike the rest, he will not resign himself to habit. He's in love. He has a new destiny now. Things have changed. He swears this to himself, just as if he were swearing it to another, *the* Other, the one who was with the young woman last night. And that Other is so different from the milquetoast office worker who now hurries along the avenue toward the subway.

At this hour, as everyone marches off to work, guerrilla attacks are more common and the subway is sometimes out of service. He worries less about the guerrilla attacks, bombs, poison gas filtering through subway cars and tunnels than he does about arriving late to the office.

Flames rise on the opposite corner. First fire, then an explosion. A military truck bursts into fragments. The shock wave is deafening. Auto parts and human remains levitate into the air. Shards, limbs, blood. A cloud of metal, plastic, glass, and flesh rises and falls, scattering over the fallen, the wounded men and women. All those who witness the attack are dazed. But he keeps going. In a few minutes the avenue will be blocked by the army and by ambulances.

He hopes the young woman will be unharmed.

15

THE ARMY CONTROLS THE SUBWAY ENTRANCE. They ask to see his papers; they pat him down. All he needs now is for them to take him for a guerrilla and move him to a secret detention center, torture him, and then throw him into the sea from a plane. These days you just can't tell who's a subversive and who's an ordinary citizen. They return his papers. He can pass. He counts out the coins for his ride. All his life he's counted coins. If he were rich, he'd quit his job, leave his family, and, of course, run away with the young woman. He'd buy her a dental implant. When he thinks about fate, as he does now, he fantasizes about a stroke of luck or daring. The lottery, or embezzlement. In his case, he thinks, luck was always against him, and the temptation of robbery never became more than a desperate fantasy.

Not very far away, just a few meters, stands his office mate. Neatly dressed, with damp hair, reading a book. He didn't know the other man was a reader. In fact, he doesn't know him at all except for the fact that he keeps a diary. The clerk steps back and blends in with those who are waiting for the train at the other end of the platform. He doesn't want to find himself in the situation of having an awkward conversation with his colleague. Even in superficial chitchat you always reveal some detail about yourself, a crack opening to the other person's curiosity. The less you know about another person, he tells himself, the less the other person will know about you. Luckily, the clamor of an approaching train emerges from the depths of the tunnel.

He rides squeezed between men and women numbed with sleep. Pressed against them, he has no need to grab a strap to keep his balance as the car, screeching, lurches ahead at full speed in the blackness of the tunnel, sparking against the rails. Between shoves and balancing acts, he's one more body among bodies. Cattle to the slaughterhouse. Future sides of beef. Maybe the guerrillas are right to attack subways: it's the most efficient way to eliminate those who refuse to face their destiny. Though if a bomb were to go off today on this train, spreading gas throughout the cars and the tunnel and exterminating the passengers, today, he would be sorry. Because today he's not just one more passenger; he's not the same as yesterday; he's not the one he used to be, and he's learned a lesson. Love has taught him that he can change. He's realized that he can be someone else. And that someone else, among all others, feels superior.

He blends in with the multitude that emerges from the subway car, elbowing one another. His office mate, up ahead, can see him; he struggles to get ahead of the crowd. The clerk, on the other hand, wants to stay back. He's the last one to get on the escalator, ride to the surface, and step into the morning. There's not a big difference between the artificial light of the subway and the daylight. The city is shrouded in a cloud of fumes that grows gummy in the acid drizzle. Silhouettes, profiles, outlines. High up, atop the buildings, caryatids, gargoyles, and cupulas vanish into threads of fog. The noise of helicopters, their blades. They aren't visible, but they're up there, always, those helicopters. He walks with his head down, sunk between the lapels of his overcoat. Tiles, concrete, asphalt, tiles again. He steps around a puddle, a few trash cans, and keeps going. He avoids some cloned dogs that lunge at him, a panhandler, Salvation Army workers in uniform. There are plenty of people distributing flyers for computer businesses, a delivery service, a sauna, intensive English courses, pretty girls, all sorts of promotions. As he crosses an avenue, the light turns red and he is forced to stop on a median. Cars whizz by him, splash him. When he finally crosses, he turns the corner, and—eyes still lowered—continues on his way.

He passes a group of men and women who are making a racket over a spectacle. It's nothing new to see an indigenous woman giving birth. Those Indians give birth all the time. All the time and everywhere. And yet, the scene doesn't fail to attract attention.

The growing audience witnesses the birth as if it were a street art performance. In front of the woman a blanket is spread out with little plastic bags containing a variety of herbs and spices. Pepper, garlic powder, oregano, sesame, sage, bay leaves, thyme, saffron, chamomile, lime flower. Next to the woman there is also a can filled with coins and wrinkled bills. Eventually, he thinks, the Indians will reign again on this continent. They never stop breeding. The Indian woman is unperturbed. Short, squat, almond-eyed, a coil of black hair, she's like a clay statue. She bears the pain, resists the suffering of her contractions. She pushes again and again. She pushes, and the baby begins to emerge from inside her. She pushes. Brief spasms. Streams of blood and amniotic fluid. She pushes. She severs the cord with her teeth. She picks up the dark, purplish child.

But not everyone watches the spectacle unmoved. A pregnant blonde, probably a secretary, faints. A man feels dizzy and moves away. Others, stumbling over one another, run off to vomit. A boy breaks down. An old woman protests. Several step back, frightened. Somebody calls for an ambulance. The clerk stands before the Indian woman. A siren sounds. The curious onlookers make way for the ambulance. A paramedic leaps out of the cab and two nurses follow her. They lower a stretcher. The public opens rank for the nurses. The paramedic bends over the pregnant blonde, who doesn't respond, takes her pulse, checks her with a stethoscope, turns, makes a sign to the nurses.

On the sidewalk, everyone turns their back on the Indian. The blonde, pregnant woman, the paramedic, and the nurses have captured the audience's attention. Now he's the only one left standing intrepidly by the Indian woman, looking her in the eye. The woman wraps the infant in a poncho, cradles him in her arms. Then she takes some sheets of newspaper from a bag, and, still holding the child in one arm, cleans around herself, scrubbing. She scrubs and looks at him. He doesn't like the way the woman smells, but he smiles at her anyway.

Everyone watches the paramedic as she examines the pregnant blonde. The nurses settle her on the stretcher, lift it into the ambulance, and take her away.

Then he disappears into the swarm of men and women hurrying to carry out their daily routines, while overhead the bells of a nearby church begin to ring.

16

AS HE APPROACHES THE OFFICE, he buys a chocolate candy from a kiosk. He reproaches himself for never buying one for El Viejito. He mustn't think about El Viejito now. Now he's someone else. And that someone has no pity. Pity undermines you. The other person he's become is beyond pity. The Other knows that beggars, for example, are as annoying as they are necessary. Annoying, because they get in your way, they stink, and they're scary: they're what you might turn into tomorrow. Direct, non-stop. They're necessary, because their presence allows for charity: a little spare change is enough to make you feel like a philanthropist. Other people's tragedies alleviate your own. That's the truth, he says to himself, but no one wants to admit it. Sincerity gets bad press, he thinks. He counts his change, puts away the chocolate. He's happy.

He looks up. The skyscraper stretches upward, disappearing among the clouds. The clerk admires the building. With his overcoat folded over his arm, adjusting the knot of his tie, he pushes through the revolving door, becoming one more being crossing the lobby. He overflows with joy. But he must be careful. The boss, he remembers. A secretary's romantic inclinations always lead to dinner with the boss, an intimate dinner, crystal glasses, and fine wine. Then the boss's car flashes across the night highways toward a motel on the edge of town, and later, when the forbidden becomes routine, little gifts, a charming apartment. He imagines the boss panting on top of her, pumping away. Jealousy, independent of one's will, is, like love, a female thing, he repeats to himself.

He feels like a secretary.

17

THIS MORNING, BEFORE ENTERING THE OFFICE, he realizes that
a firing is about to take place. There's a smartly-dressed young man
waiting in the reception area, to one side of the main entrance to
the office. Whenever you find a young man or woman sitting beside
the large reception-room door, you know that he or she has come to
replace someone. The newcomers wait, ready to occupy a position
and spring into action while the frightened employees walk into
the room, wondering who will be replaced, who will be fired. The
young man, with his slicked-back hair, gray suit, white shirt, and
blue tie, waits next to the entrance, like a grenadier on duty.

In one instant, just as soon as everyone has taken their places,
a loudspeaker announces the name of the man or woman who's
been dismissed. In a neutral voice, like an airport announcement,
the victim's name is formally revealed. A security team surrounds
the deposed man or woman's desk, preventing any opposition to the
measure.

The clerk worries it may be his turn. He wonders if the secretary might not have told the boss that she'd gone to bed with him
last night. She could have told him out of revenge. Maybe, cleverer
still, the young woman might have told the boss that he tried to win
her away. With women you can never tell.

He has to control his nerves. He might not be the one to be
replaced just a few minutes from now. In his years of working at
an office, his whole life, he has seen presidents, vice-presidents,
directors, assistant directors, managers, assistant managers, section
leaders, vice-leaders, division executives, supervisors, secretaries,
and telephone operators parade through the building. He has seen
so many faces change. Each change, each restructuring, each new
section division, transfer, suggests a presumed transformation of the
office, hierarchies, and personnel functions. Changes of desks, panels, furniture, carpets, computers, programs, files, tables, and forms.

A change of desk, of place, proves that no one owns anything. Just as the employees don't own their desks, neither do they own their lives. If within the office they must guard their jobs by working, outside the office they must plan how to exercise caution to keep them. Every change is expected to bring about greater productivity. Excellence, service, dynamics: these are terms that the higher-ups tend to pronounce every time a change is coming. The changes translate into a relentless personnel reduction. Which can be massive or partial. If a firing occurs as an isolated incident, it's enough to cause alarm. This is a warning.

In any of these cases, it makes no sense to discuss the order that came from above. No argument will change the sentence of the superiors. Which explains why the victim meekly accepts his new reality.

Neither tears nor a tragic expression moves the security team surrounding the pariah. The ones who create the most tragicomic scenes are the women. They scratch, they bite. They're pathetic; it takes more time for the security team to subdue them. Finally, by using gags, they manage to get rid of them. The newer hires aren't any less ridiculous: they try to resist, as if the decree could be reversed. No matter how tightly they cling to their desks, their efforts are useless. The security team intervenes, immediately dissolving the dismissed worker's rebellion. It's pathetic when someone cries, kicks, and thrashes, while they're held down by the wrists and ankles and carried to one of the freight elevators in the rear. You can still hear their screams. Then, finally, the metallic echo of the elevator.

And what if it was his office mate's turn, he asks himself. It would bring him great joy if that were the case. He imagines the other man clutching his desk, refusing to abandon his spot, as the security guards yank him away. As he struggles, his office mate drops his notebook. And he doesn't miss his chance. He picks it up, hides it away. He prays for this to happen. Though praying for a misfortune to befall somebody is a sacrilege. He recites the Our Father in his head.

The loudspeakers pronounce a name. And the victim stands. He's a few desks away. Like everybody else, the clerk avoids looking at the fired man. It breaks his heart to look at him. And yet, someone else's misfortune works like a consolation. It was another person's turn. Now, a temporary calm. Like everyone else, like anyone else, when he casts a sidelong glance at the fired man, he thinks that when it's his turn, he won't make a scene.

In a few moments, the empty desk will be occupied by the newcomer who's been waiting in the reception area.

The old-timers, those who have seen the most firings, seem more resigned. But they still can't get accustomed to the possibility that they might be next. No matter how they try to feign a certain blasé air, the old-timers can't stand the idea of being disposable, the notion that it might be their turn to be touched by the oft-repeated tragedy. In the long run, whenever there's a firing, no one can keep working without feeling anxious. And if that weren't enough, the anxiety is dangerous. Because nerves can lead you to make a mistake at work, a mistake that might lead you to be the next one replaced.

It also happens that when the employees notice the new man or woman waiting, they greet them with a smile, a wink, a formal nod, because the newcomer, in a very short while, may occupy a nearby desk, and it's not a good idea to start off on the wrong foot. It's better to be a little diplomatic, wait till a reasonable time has passed in order to calculate how much rivalry is presented by the adjacent desk.

This morning's victim, surrounded by the security team, standing before his desk, stroking it delicately, like someone bidding farewell to a casket containing a loved one. Then the victim looks around. Everyone avoids his eyes. They would be crushed, if they noticed tears in his eyes. If they want to finish out the day, they can't give in to pity. To look at the victim is to look backward. One mustn't look backward. What happened to the victim, his firing, can't be helped. Let them take him away. Let him disappear once and for all. The victim doesn't want to look defeated. He smiles, takes a plastic bag from a drawer and starts filling it with his personal effects. The security team checks the bag, watching each item the victim takes with him. Personal effects only: not one paper clip. They grab him by the arm and take him away. Before the victim leaves the room, he crosses paths with the newcomer heading for his former spot.

Once these activities are concluded, the changes reveal their true objective: for things to go on as usual. Nevertheless, the youngest employees, power-crazed by a salary raise, a promotion, take every change seriously. There was a time when he, too, took such changes seriously. But now the only thing that matters to him is keeping his job. He grasps his desk firmly, lowers his head, and waits for the wind to blow through.

He can't attribute this morning's anguish only to last night. The firing that took place so close to him also weighs on his spirit. And that's not even counting the fact that his workplace demands have increased. Because for a while now, with the goal of streamlining bureaucracy at the office, holidays, weekends, and vacations have been eliminated. A new filing system has been created, but the change causes the opposite result: the new files are more cumbersome, expanding by the hour, and there aren't enough employees to handle them. Millions of files could not be entered into the computer system. And the system, in turn, sometimes breaks down due to the electrical outages caused by attacks.

That's how it is: those who aren't office zealots will be added to the next lists and join the bands of ragged homeless who sleep on the street. Because the employees regard these scavengers with scorn, a scorn in which you can read terror: tomorrow, following a decision by the higher-ups, they might be those ghosts who will return their disdainful glances, but with a different kind of scorn: that of those who have already seen themselves at their lowest ebb. He needs to tame these wild imaginings. The morning still looms darkly through the windows. The acid rain grows denser. The foggy sky brings back the night. The office is illuminated with fluorescent bulbs, desk lamps, and the radiation emanating from the computers. His office mate, already at his desk, is sorting files. The secretary's computer is on, but she isn't at her desk. Cautiously, turning his back to his colleague, he leaves the chocolate on the secretary's desk, and then, beaming, he sits down at his station, and turns on his computer.

Opposite the desks are the offices of each section director. The ranking personnel communicates with the ordinary workers with a bland cordiality that includes the use of the familiar *tú*. If someone needs to leave his desk for some reason, he picks up a folder, some papers. No one leaves his place without pretending to be very busy. That is called professionalism. And professionalism allows for no errors. Under no condition. If it's a question of a computer error, the error can be attributed to its operator. If his machine fails him this morning, more than an unforeseen accident, it's a sign that maybe things aren't going as well as he had hoped.

The computer glitch exasperates him, but not as much as the secretary's absence. Why isn't she at her desk, he wonders.

18

ALL THE WOMEN, ALL THE MEN, plugged into their computers. You can hardly hear the keyboards. Every so often, the pounding of a stamp. And again, the keyboards. Before coming to the office, the workers go to a gym. Their concern for health and beauty is proportional to their fear of losing their jobs. A sick man doesn't produce. A sloppy person suggests apathy. Efficiency is what counts. All of them proud to be part of this army of desks. The men in shirts and ties and the women in blouses and skirts, all in discreet colors. They visibly demonstrate an unspoken *esprit de corps*. The clerk is sure that sometimes an attraction develops between the men and the women. It makes sense: so many hours spent shut indoors, overcome by instinct, they inevitably explode in sudden, clandestine couplings that relieve tension. If, behind a panel, in a bathroom, someone stumbles upon a man and a woman, two men or two women, two men and a woman, or two women and a man, all of them panting in a burst of passion, he'll look the other way. Even if rumors of the relationship circulate afterward, it won't go beyond that, unless it points toward a wedding. In which case one of the parties must end it, to avoid allowing marital conflicts to invade the office. In all the years he's been at the office, the clerk has never had a flirtation. Never.

He tries to relax. The computer is finally working again. He blends in with the efficiency of the rest of the personnel. It's easy for him to blend in, though his appearance doesn't convince him. If he keeps his job, it definitely won't be due to his looks. At the end of the last century, he was one of the few who knew how to adapt to the advances in technology, when computers replaced calculators and typewriters. His quick adaptation came more from fear than from his intellectual acuity. If he's held on to his job, it's been on account of his meekness, and, basically, his shrewdness in cutting down on doing things the old-fashioned way. He's become as indispensable as a file. He likes being considered as useful as a file. You can tell by that photo he displays on his desk: there he is, at an office anniversary party, receiving a bronze mouse from the boss, which he happily uses as a paperweight.

As he waits for his computer to boot up, he sharpens a pencil to calm his nerves. He writes a label for a folder. And he stamps a few records with a seal. He's about to get up and take the chocolate from the secretary's desk. He feels ridiculous. He looks at the sky through a window: a mouse-gray canvas. Again that lightheadedness. He wonders how brave he'd have to be to charge against the window, leap headfirst, break through the void in an explosion of glass. He's thought about suicide before, but now it seems imminent to him. He has to hang on. Rigidity bolts him in place; his jaw contracts. If he doesn't loosen up, he thinks, his gums will start to bleed.

The secretary emerges from the boss's office. She's carrying some folders. This morning she's wearing a tailored blue suit. She walks with resolve, elegance. She's not a secretary. She's a flight attendant. She discovers the chocolate on her desk, and, turning, she gives the clerk a conspiratorial wink. But he doesn't let himself be fooled: she's just come out of the boss's office. The zipper of her skirt is partly open. When she crosses her legs, he notices that one stocking has an almost imperceptible tear. The open zipper and a run in one stocking. Two clear signs of what took place in the boss's office.

She unwraps the chocolate, takes a bite. She tastes it. Teasingly she sticks out the tip of her tongue, licks her lips. She looks at him suggestively. Deceitfully, he thinks.

And he turns around. Because it's a sure thing his office mate is capturing these gestures in his notebook. In fact, when he turns around, the other man, with that little smile, like a child caught in the act, puts the notebook away.

The fact that the computer is up again is a positive sign, he tells himself. Though what it's a sign of, he doesn't know. Futilely he tries to concentrate on work. He types like a robot. She spies on him from her desk. He thinks there's kindness in that expression behind the round glasses, but it could be a trap. He stands, says excuse me. He has no reason to excuse himself, but he does it anyway. He walks toward the door, crosses the corridor, goes into the bathroom, makes sure there's nobody else there, and locks himself in a stall.

Standing, resting one hand on the tiles, he masturbates like crazy.

19

WHEN HE RETURNS, AGITATED, TO HIS DESK, the secretary tells him that the boss wants to see him. Everything that's happened to him this morning is her fault, he says to himself. What happened last night was unforgivable. It wasn't love. It was sex. Just sex. And he, like an idiot, let himself be charmed by a social climber, using him to cushion her loneliness after an argument with her lover. She's evaluated what she had to lose by breaking up with the boss, that slut. This morning she hurried to the office early and made up with him. It's very clear: regretful about the night before, she'll want to be rid of him. Her next move will be to get him fired. He's got to watch out for this unscrupulous woman who now, in a neutral tone—as if nothing ever happened here—tells him that the boss has asked for the checks.

Among his administrative tasks, the checks are one of his greatest responsibilities. Because of his seniority at the office, he has been deemed the right one to analyze budgets, determine payments. All office accounting comes through his desk. The clerk studies it in detail. After that, the boss barely looks at the papers. Since he trusts his employee, he often signs them confidently, without paying much attention. The same thing happens with the checks.

In the boss's office, with its windows framing the dark clouds, the only source of light comes from the desk lamp. Only the boss's huge hands and his impressive ring are visible. The rest of his body is in shadow. Anyone entering this office feels inferior. It must have happened to the young woman, he thinks. The boss must have taken advantage of her fragility. He feels the young woman's submission in his own body. The boss fondling him, pulling down his pants, his underwear, twisting him forward on top of the desk, his ass in the air, and he, clutching the edges of the desk while the other man, with one hand on his neck and another at his waist, penetrates him.

The boss has a silver-framed photo on his desk: he and his family in front of a chalet. Here you can see the boss with his loved ones, a classically beautiful blonde, and the children, who are also blonde. A little boy and a girl. In the photo you can see the family's high social status on display. Still imagining himself in the young woman's place, as the boss possesses him, face down on the desk, and simultaneously feeling as though he, too, has been nailed into the same position, his naked butt in the air, the boss's prominent belly on top of him, his pants down around his ankles, a sharp pain in his anus, his cheek pressed against the desk. He looks at the family photo. Slowly he's overcome by a pleasurable feeling of abandon. He feels the stream of semen. What humiliates him most is feeling the boss's stream trigger his own. The boss's orgasm makes him explode.

He looks at the family photo and closes his eyes. The terrible thing is not that the boss may have mounted the young woman. The terrible thing is that she may have enjoyed it.

He reproaches himself for thinking about this filth. A man in love should be idealistic, a dreamer.

He wonders what kind of love he feels.

20

THE BOSS IS READING SOME DOCUMENTS. He ignores the subordinate standing at his desk. The clerk clears his throat: his way of announcing he's there. Taking the folder with the checks, the boss hardly looks up. After a long time, he notices him. He asks him, point blank, what he thinks of that photo of his family. The clerk stammers. He can't think of what to say. An ideal family, he thinks. He'd rather have the boss reprimand him for a mistake than have to answer such a loaded question. He asks him to say what he sees in the photo, what he thinks of his family. The boss has probably been charged with a new reduction in personnel. He's testing him to determine just how far his toadying will go. He's gone through these paranoid episodes before, when a sibylline rumor hangs over the desks and turns colleagues into enemies. Every glance, every gesture: a warning. Treason lurking behind every desk. He knows how to hang on to his desk until the firings are over. However, he can never let himself be distracted. Mass dismissals bulldoze through the office when you least expect it.

The boss picks up the photo, studies it. Then, with a sad expression, he touches his bald spot and remarks that his children's hair will never fall out. Take a good look at the kids in the picture. Just compare those kids' hair with my bald spot, he says. They have hair, the boss says. And they're blonde. Lots of hair, and blonde, too. The boss asks if he has any idea why his kids' hair isn't going to fall out. The clerk falls silent. It's a very delicate situation. Whatever reply he chooses, in addition to being spontaneous, will have to be obliging but not brown-nosing. At last the clerk ventures an opinion. The children haven't suffered their father's stress yet, he says. Because being a boss, in his opinion, being in this place, holding a position with so much responsibility, must be exhausting. That's what he thinks, at least.

The boss isn't satisfied with his response. Don't feel sorry for me,

[52]

he says. If his children have blonde hair and lots of it, there's a different reason. Balkan. Imported. After a series of tests, it turned out his wife was sterile. The couple decided to adopt. They preferred Balkan babies over little Indian ones. Imported, the boss repeats. Blonde. He and his wife chose blondes.

Adoption is a truly charitable act, the clerk says. He speaks of its nobility.

But the praise has no effect.

The boss strokes his forehead, his receding hairline, his bald spot, and smiles bitterly. Maybe later he'll decide to kill him for knowing too much, the clerk suspects. If he's revealed the story of his children to him, the boss explains, it's because he considers him intelligent. Sometimes, the boss confesses, he feels so alone. The loneliness of power, he says. Naturally he suggests discretion on the subject.

The boss signs the checks without reviewing them. The clerk waits silently. He doesn't know what to say. The boss hands him the folder with the checks; the clerk looks at him. This must be the first time he's held the boss's gaze. He needs to say something, but he can't think of what. A wise statement that might be applied as comforting in any unfortunate situation. He likes to keep a repertory of phrases on hand. Proverbs, aphorisms, quotes by famous people. They often help him out of a sticky situation when he doesn't know what to say. That's what happens when you're a common-sense kind of guy. Nothing less common than common sense, as the old saying goes. You don't have to be a superstar to get out of a tough spot. Just tight-lipped and basic. He mutters a proverb. The boss looks at him, looks at him and touches his bald spot again, rubbing it and meditating, meditating and smiling, smiling and saying thank you. The clerk leaves the office, his shirt clinging to his back.

The secretary walks up to him and asks him if everything's all right. And he, not knowing what "everything" and "all right" are, nods. She asks what he's doing at lunchtime, if he'd like to have lunch together. She's taken the lead again. Now, more than ever, he must be cautious. Though from the way she talks to him, she's once more the young ingénue. He wonders which of the two she is: the girl from last night or the one who until recently was behind closed doors with the boss.

We're all someone else, he thinks.

21

AT NOON THE DOWNTOWN AREA IS AN ANTHILL. As the couple emerges from the building, the crowd envelops them. They walk along the avenue and turn onto a pedestrian street. At each corner, military trucks, riot control brigades, teams with helmets, bullet-proof vests, tear-gas guns, machine guns, and attack dogs. The acid rain has diminished, but the day is still foggy. In spite of the brightly-lit businesses and shop windows, it feels like night, a sensation reinforced by the helicopter searchlights focusing here and there, preventing groups from gathering. Four or five people getting together might be enough to start a demonstration. One group here, another there, a few more, suddenly they start shouting, converging, and throwing grenades at buildings. The most dangerous ones are the suicide guerrillas who walk into a bank, a ministry, or a restaurant loaded with explosives. Then the downtown area becomes a combat zone. A mass of desperate people seeking refuge amid deafening explosions and gunfire. Shrieks, stampedes, barking, gas, flames, rubble, scraps of metal, mutilated bodies. If there's a disturbance, he'll pull the young woman toward shelter, and, without wasting the opportunity, in his zeal to protect her, he'll embrace her and kiss her. But today there are no new developments on the downtown front. And he can't flaunt his heroism. He has to be satisfied with being friendly.

The city has its bluish tones. Neon signs and traffic lights twinkle, the colorful glow of shop windows. There is a luminous shimmer between the smoke from the exhaust pipes and the dust that rises and expands from the excavations that squads of indigenous workers work on ceaselessly. Pits, ditches, holes. The laying of subway lines in the city remains uninterrupted. If the Indians' ancestors raised pyramids, now their descendants dig beneath the earth, the clerk observes. The secretary says he's very observant.

He smiles with pleasure. The coming and going of men and women, the roaring, rushing traffic, the thunder of engines and machinery are compounded by the screech of tires, police sirens, voices of the crowd, the clamor of street vendors, and, often, the music of the Andean highlands, played by a trio of Indians with ponchos, *quenas*, *charangos*, and *bombos*. The couple turns onto another pedestrian street. Despite the crowds, in this gorge of concrete and cement, the city sounds are muted, like those of an enclosed courtyard.

They enter a lunch place decorated with artificial plants and ferns in gold-painted flowerpots, an attempt to soften the coldness of plastic, Formica, acrylic. The place has a tropical feel. Photos of platters and dishes of food, desserts, and fruit, arranged in panels, alternate with menus and TV screens blaring the news: looting, kidnappings, murders, protests, building takeovers, hooded mobs facing off against attack vehicles, grenades, pandemonium. At a school a twelve-year-old girl shot her teacher and her entire class. The clerk pays close attention to this news item. It's not the school his kids attend. The diners form a line in front of the counters and the containers of food. The clatter of dishes and the nervous voices of the waitresses behind the counter muffle the background music. A bolero. He knows the words. He whispers them to the young woman: a few verses about sin and punishment.

The two of them, one next to the other, among the hungry crowd searching for trays and cutlery. Then they walk up to the counters where the food awaits. For her, a chicken leg with pureed squash. For him, roast lamb with potatoes. They help themselves to mineral water.

On the TV screens, roads, grasslands, the poverty of the multitudes, an ambulance, paramedics. On board a train, some kids relieved an old man of his pension check and then threw him onto the rails. The old man was run over by a train coming from the opposite direction. The camera zooms in on his mutilated body, the torso on one side, the legs on the other, an arm a few meters away, a foot. Firefighters collect the pieces scattered all around and place them on a stretcher.

Now the two of them, sitting at a table, eat and look at one another. They chew with their mouths closed. They dab their lips with a paper napkin before drinking water. She, with those little eyeglasses in which he sees his reflection, combines innocence with a mischievous self-assurance. This can't be the face of a social climber, he thinks.

Farther down, at another table, they see their office mate. He's reading and writing as he eats. Between mouthfuls of meat pie, concentrating intensely, he appears to be copying what he reads into the notebook. He looks at the book and then writes. Again and again. The two of them notice their office mate at the same time and watch him without saying anything. Neither has the courage to comment. He's afraid that she'll get the notion of inviting him to share the table, but she doesn't. She's careful not to say what she thinks of their colleague, and this discretion of hers, he thinks, won't be without a price. It's a well-known fact that any insulting remark about someone at the office is a three-forked tongue: it hurts the speaker, it hurts the listener, and it hurts the victim. Ignoring their colleague, as if that reminder of the office wasn't there, they turn back to their conversation. But the words have lost their spontaneity. He'd swear both of them are thinking the same thing: the sight of their office mate, the same alarm. Seeing them together could lead to suspicions. And what if it wasn't a coincidence, he wonders, that the colleague chose that particular place to have lunch.

They talk about food. She likes Japanese food. He prefers Italian. The fact that she likes Japanese puts him on guard. It must've been the boss who introduced her to Japanese cuisine, a real seduction strategy. Thinking about the boss makes him choke. He needs a drink of water to breathe normally. She asks him if he's tried Thai food. He shakes his head no. The farthest he's gone in his culinary journeys was to China. Cantonese, he says. And what about

Mexican food, he asks her. No, she's never tried it. She heard it was spicy. Spicy food doesn't agree with her, she says. She blushes. She's been operated on, she says. No need for further explanation. One night he'll invite her to a French restaurant. He says so and stares at her, waiting. She cuts the chicken leg. She tells him she can tell he's a sensitive person. Captivated, he draws on all his cleverness to display whatever he knows about history and geography. For example, noodles. Marco Polo brought them back from the Far East. He tells her about the voyages of Marco Polo and later digresses with a story about the Silk Road. He's about to turn north, toward Siberian gold, but he cuts himself off. He asks her if she's bored. Not at all—it's fascinating, she replies. Every day you learn something new; she adores everything he knows. He bows his head humbly. She never would have imagined that, so close by, at that desk, there sat such a spiritual person. Flattered, he says that she shouldn't put him on a pedestal. She asks if he cooks. This is a good opportunity for him to talk about himself, about his unhappy marriage, but it would sound like a typical adulterer's device. She looks at him. He can't sustain that gaze: it calls attention to him. He's embarrassed. He turns toward the table where the office mate was having lunch. He's left without the clerk having noticed.

She loves curry and soy sauce, she says.

They fall silent. They fall silent and look at one another. They look at one another and lower their eyes. Then he looks at a TV set and she looks at what he's looking at. Some kids on the street resisted arrest by the police. A young girl with a pocketknife struggles with two policewomen who corner her against a wire fence. The policewomen beat her into submission with their clubs, handcuff her, and shove her into a police car. The camera focuses on her bloodied face, the red puddle on the concrete. When the news bulletin ends, they look at one another again. They remain silent. Neither of them speaks of what happened to them last night.

Until he can't stand it anymore and tells her what he thinks, that they need to talk about last night. Because what he felt last night, he confesses, he's never felt before. On the TV screens, some cars are burning at the side of a deserted road, dark clouds of smoke, bodies scattered here and there as firefighters and paramedics run around. She says that it's not necessary to think of what happened as falling in love. His love isn't any less real, he replies, just because it was sudden. Ever since daybreak, when they said goodnight, he hasn't done anything but think of her. Right now, in fact, he can't wait until he can be with her again. Hopelessly in love, he tells her, that's what he is. She listens. She listens and eats. She eats, and only the chicken bone remains on the dish. Not a trace of the puréed squash. He's hardly touched a bite of his lunch, she says. He regards his plate sadly. The meat has grown cold. She points out the potatoes. He really should eat the potatoes. He smiles. Love takes away a person's appetite. He realizes he shouldn't persist with his declaration. He sees her sitting on their boss's lap, telling him about this lunch, about his profession of love. She imitates him. They both burst out laughing. Laughing at him. Still laughing, she kneels before the boss, takes his penis and puts it in her mouth. The boss grabs her head.

And what if this were just another one of his fantasies, he asks himself.

He drinks more water.

22

LUNCH HOUR FLIES BY. He wonders if this sensation of time slipping away is just his imagination. They stand, walk between the diners, make their way to the cash register. He rushes ahead to pay. She objects. He insists. Split it down the middle, she suggests. This refusal, he thinks, could be a female gesture, but it could also be a rejection. He can't avoid feeling frustrated. Suddenly it occurs to him that giving her flowers would be the right thing to do. He wonders which flowers she likes. But, he reflects, if he gives her flowers now everyone will make remarks when they get back to the office. He needs to wait, he thinks. He'll have a chance to get back to it in the afternoon. He's not going let the night go by, and when he thinks of the night, he thinks of the word as a Caribbean bolero singer would pronounce it: *nochie*.

As he walks out into the street—helicopters. When they fly so low it's because something is about to happen, he says. He takes her by the arm; they walk hurriedly along the stretch leading to the office. They've barely crossed the corridor when, behind them, an explosion shakes the building. The shockwave, the din plugging their ears. He pushes her toward the elevator. Run, he shouts. Don't stop, he says. The attack took place on the street, opposite them. From the street: screams, gunshots, bricks, wailing, sirens, chaos. An avalanche of personnel rushes toward the elevators. The elevator doors close; they're squeezed in among other employees. Someone smiles hysterically. Someone is about to throw up. And someone shits his pants. She thanks him for his protective instinct.

They settle down at their desks, take up their work again. The office mate's desk is still empty. The clerk is suddenly seized with the hope that he died in the explosion. It would be such a relief if he had been killed. He imagines the firefighters and first responders gathering his colleague's remains, an arm here, some guts there, over there, a foot. But no: his office mate arrives shortly afterward. He brushes the dust from his shoulders and sits down at his desk.

If God exists, the clerk thinks, he'll have to get this guy off my back.

23

FROM NOW UNTIL THE END OF THE WORKDAY, he'll have to contain his passion. And also be alert to his colleague's stare, a stare he can feel on the back of his neck. He turns around: his office mate seems to be concentrating on his work. He lifts his head from a file and flashes him that little smile.

Just like the previous morning at daybreak, when he left the young woman's apartment and started counting the seconds that separated him from this day, he now begins to count them again. Mouth dry as sand, palms sweaty, heart pounding. Get a handle on this anxiety, he says to himself. He can't. He grabs a notepad. He jots down every phrase of the conversation at the luncheonette. What she said to him, everything she said to him. Each phrase lends itself to different interpretations. He jots it all down, phrase after phrase. He also makes notes of what the young woman's reactions were. She smiled, he writes. She sighed, he writes. She remained silent, he writes. His notes, he discovers, resemble an intimate diary. He thinks of his office mate and his notebook. It makes him tremble to think that he had been breeding contempt for the other man for so long, and only now does he realize that, so close to him, at that neighboring desk, is someone who could be his friend. He feels dizzy with the desire to throw himself on his colleague and tell him everything, to open up his heart and confess his misery, and also how, poisoned by jealousy, he had mistrusted him, thinking he was an enemy. Surely, confronted with an open heart, his colleague will embrace him. But it doesn't take him long to come to his senses. It might be premature to air his innermost feelings, he thinks. This may be another of his fantasies.

Then, looking over a pile of folios, he sees the young woman. The only thing missing to torment the rest of his afternoon would be for the boss to summon her into his office. The young woman's phone rings. She picks up. Then, carrying some files, she walks into the boss's office.

He counts the minutes. The minutes turn into an hour. The hours, a calvary. All the employees begin to leave. His office mate, too. See you tomorrow, he says. The clerk barely returns his wave. If he were brave, he thinks, he'd march into the office right now, and even if she was on all fours with the boss riding her, he'd assert himself: those two would find out who he really is. But, he wonders, how is he supposed to show them his strength if he doesn't know himself. The windows grow dark, and in the twilight the employees continue to leave. The office, deserted. The secretary, still in the boss's office.

Finally, he makes up his mind. Too humiliating, he thinks. He can't take it anymore. He turns off the computer. He picks up his coat, puts it on, and walks away: the corridor, the elevator, he descends. The silence of the building. It's drizzling now. After the attack, the front entrance is protected by partitions. Some workers carry away debris in a dump truck. He continues on his way. At the corner, he stops, flips up his collar, and goes into a phone booth. He admonishes himself for not having asked the young woman for her cell phone number. He lifts the receiver, making sure there's a dial tone, inserts a few coins, dials. He listens to the office's recorded message, dials the boss's extension. No one answers. What those two must be doing right now. He hangs up and calls again. He calls the young woman's extension. On the other end, the phone rings, rings, rings, and rings. It keeps ringing as he sees a car emerge from the building's parking garage. It's the boss's car. It passes by the phone booth. He shrinks. There she is, curled up against the boss.

Without letting go of the receiver, he slips down to the floor of the phone booth. With the phone next to his ear, he cries, listening to the unanswered ringing in the deserted office.

24

LATELY, AS DUSK FALLS, a heavy drowsiness begins to overtake him. When he feels it coming, he nods off. He looks around. No one has noticed his sleepiness, his sudden fatigue. The exhaustion. Luckily no one took notice of that nod. The secretary's desk is still empty. Many of his colleagues are turning off their computers, locking their desk drawers, saying goodbye until tomorrow. But not him. Tonight he won't abandon his post as long as she's still in the office. He will not tolerate a humiliation like the night before, when she left with the boss. If she plans to go off with the boss, they'll have to walk by his desk first. Then he'll nail her with a look. Let's see if she has the nerve to stare him down.

He pores over a file, reviews the checks again and again. Work is an escape. If only he could separate his head from his body, loosen his screws and analyze his circuits, his connections. He imagines himself as a robot that's able to repair itself, one that can remove its own head, and, by putting it on top of the desk, with the help of screwdrivers and pliers, can loosen one piece after another and adapt the conduits through which desire flows. The headless mechanical doll places its head on the desk, checks a valve, changes a burnt-out fuse, reconnects two cables, and repairs its own mechanism. Then, when it returns the head to its proper place, readjusting it to the body, it feels satisfied: no desire, no matter how unbridled, will affect its normal functioning.

But desperation wins out. An unbearable headache. His eyes grown cloudy, his mouth as dry as a desert, his palms sweaty. Rapid heartbeat, dizziness, and nausea. He stands slowly, with feigned ease. He goes to the bathroom. And in the bathroom he loosens his shirt collar, rolls up the sleeves, wets his wrists, his face, and then swallows some aspirin. Every time this happens to him, he avoids looking in the mirror. But after a long moment, he starts to enjoy his image in the mirror: a dark pleasure attracts him. The strong man isn't one who returns blows, but one who absorbs them, he tells himself.

His other self is right. If his weakness is his strength, he will use it to make the secretary change her mind, out of pity. The young woman will feel so sorry for him that she'll end up surrendering to him. He thinks about a famous blind singer, about his success with women. If the blind guy has that charm, it's not because of his irritating, subway-singer's voice. It's because of his blindness. The defect guarantees his power. But he is neither blind nor a singer. He's lame. He doesn't think he can use his limp to show off with a waltz. He checks the time.

The office. She's still there. Both of them are still there.

25

DEFEATED, HE RETURNS TO HIS LAIR. As he rides the subway, the only passenger at this hour, he reads a science magazine, as usual. If anyone were to ask him what attracts him about these magazines, he'd answer that it's the search for truth through experiments, the idea that things are not just the product of chance, that there are laws, rules, a logic that justifies everything that happens in the universe. Everything that happens under heaven must have an explanation. But instead of bringing him peace, all explanations generate new unknowns. By accumulating information about all sorts of phenomena, he sometimes plunges even more deeply into bleak ruminations. His is a rational spirit, he tells himself. Example: He's not ashamed of his own paranoia, because he read in an article that in their delirium, paranoiacs are at least partly right. Nothing that happens to him is without justification. But he still can't explain to himself why everything that happens to him has to happen to *him*. It's not fair, he says to himself.

If he believed in astrology, he says to himself, his existence would be more bearable. If it's true that fortune is written in the stars, if it's possible to predict the future, he could predict the facts, know the circumstances, when to act or when to keep still. But an article robbed him of this illusion. An experiment carried out in Manchester. Scientists closely followed the development of a few babies who were born on the same day, at the same time. They followed them for several years. And they came to the conclusion that each of the babies, now adolescents, had turned out different from the rest. The stars hadn't influenced the direction of their lives at all. Each one pointed to a different destiny. Heaven, it was proved, is not responsible for our successes and failures.

If only he could believe that all his pain has an explanation, a meaning, he muses as he falls asleep.

The magazine falls from his hands.

26

One evening, in the silence of the deserted office, he hears the sound of a pen scratching behind him. Then, the feet of a chair scraping across the floor. The office mate has also stayed after work. He asks the clerk if he wants a coffee; he'll bring him one. The clerk hesitates. Why not, he thinks. Ever since he became aware that he, too, could carry a diary, even though he doesn't, he's felt better about his colleague. Maybe it's not such a strange idea that, in this battle of everyone against everyone and every man for himself, the two of them might be spiritual twins. Who knows what woes trouble his colleague. He checks his pocket watch. He tells his office mate not to go to any trouble. And he follows him to the coffee maker.

The peace of the surroundings enfolds them. And even though they're the only two left at this late hour, they still speak in hushed voices. He doesn't know how to break the ice. Why not be direct, he says to himself. He asks his office mate if he wouldn't rather be with his family than here at the office. He has no family, the office mate replies. And he pauses. Then, with a happy expression, he says that at the moment he has no family, not at the moment, he emphasizes, but soon he will. Because he and his fiancée are planning to move far from the city, very far, to Patagonia. The two of them are saving to build a future together in a promised land. Because Patagonia is healing, he says. In Patagonia you can start from scratch.

He looks for his billfold. He pulls out a photo. This is his fiancée, he says. She's a red-haired girl with light-colored eyes, angular, delicate, but whose style, the clerk notices, could also reflect a devilish streak. She's wearing a dark gas-station uniform and enormous black gloves. She's standing next to a gas pump. The dark uniform emphasizes the fiery color of her hair. She must have a temper, he thinks. If he saw her at work, the office mate says, he'd see what she's like. She pumps gas, measures oil, checks air in the tires, cleans windshields. She knows a lot about mechanics. It's hard work. But it doesn't faze her. No matter how hard the work or how tired she is, she never stops smiling. She saves up all her tips. Character is important, his office mate says. You've got to have it in order to work hard. But, also, she's got the will. That's what he likes best about the girl: she accomplishes everything she sets out to do. The clerk hands him back the photo. Besides being persistent, the girl is very mystical. Maybe tenacity and mysticism go together. He talks about his fiancée with pride. He, too, makes sacrifices. The two of them rent a hole-in-the-wall on the outskirts, in a distant neighborhood. And there are days when he saves bus and subway fare by walking both ways. Walking keeps you in shape. On other days he skips lunch. Then he goes to the service station, which isn't far from the office, has a coffee at the 24-hour store, and from his table watches the girl breaking her hump among the cars. Every so often, from the pumps, she blows him a kiss. Madly in love, that's what they are. Once they've saved enough money to buy an old truck, they'll convert it into a house on wheels and travel down south; they'll settle down on government land in a valley among hills and mountains, he says. They'll build a cabin, have a small farm, they'll have kids, lots of kids, they'll live off the land, and each of them will do their own thing: she farming, he writing. Because he's a writer, he confesses. He's deeply into Russian literature, he explains. He's studied the language and the Cyrillic alphabet, he says. And he asks the clerk if he's read the Russians. No, the clerk hasn't read the Russians. His passion is scientific journals. The more science advances in its research on the human being, the more it distances itself from knowledge of the soul. Because as we get closer to truth, we get closer to pain. Instead of bringing him peace of mind, he says, scientific journals make him feel more like a microbe. The Russians, his colleague says. He must read the Russians. His eyes are moist. The Russians know about inner truth. His colleague looks like he's on the brink of tears. That's his dream, he says. To delve deeply into the Russians. A dream that he hasn't dared tell anyone, not so much for fear of being ridiculed as for fear of gossip, suspicion.

The office mate falls silent. His eyes tear up. He apologizes for having burdened the clerk with this confession. Suddenly he feels frightened. Calm down, the clerk says. There's nothing bad about his dream. Besides, he won't tell anybody, he promises. We all have a dream. Like everyone else, we have a secret. He, too, as insignificant as he may seem, has a dream. And he doesn't have the courage to tell it, either. Maybe because when we tell our dreams, if we're not up to their level, they reveal not only our vanity, but also our most secret frustrations.

He mustn't get upset, his office mate says. All men have a need for purity that drives them to breathe clean air. As proof of his friendship and also as a pact between them, the clerk says, he'll tell him about his dream. The clerk is surprised to find himself talking with the urgency and confusion of someone who was choked by guilt, even though he hasn't committed a crime. Falling in love is not a crime. And he's in love. He surprised to be telling his colleague about his family tragedy; he's surprised to be telling him about his relationship with the secretary; he's surprised to be telling him that he dreams of running away with her; he's surprised to be telling him that he can't take it anymore either. He's about to cry, too. And, as he speaks, he begins to feel that he doesn't recognize himself in the telling, that he's not the one who's speaking, but another. The Other.

His office mate embraces him. Confession unites them, he says. To plunge into confession is the essence of the Russian soul. He mustn't be afraid, he soothes him. He, too, is reserved, he says. He won't tell anybody what he's been told. With their arms flung around one another, they cry. But they don't cry for the same reason.

The clerk cries out of fear.

It would be best to figure out quickly how to eliminate his colleague.

27

HE WALKS INTO THE NIGHT. When the streets end, the open land begins. Then, the dunes.

He stops at the beach. He can barely hear the sound of the waves, a peaceful, monotonous splashing. An iceberg shifts in the night. He can see the city reflected in the ice. As he passes along the coast, the ice takes on magnificent proportions. And yet what appears on the surface is only a tiny part of the ice. What does the appearance of this floating mountain of ice mean, he wonders.

He loses track of the time he spends absorbed in contemplating the iceberg.

28

EVER SINCE THE CONFESSION, his office mate has treated him as if they were lifelong friends. With his dream of purity, the clerk thinks, his colleague must think he's a big shot. A saint in the brothel, one of those possessed souls that walks on burning coals. There's nobody more dangerous than someone who pretends to be pure, he thinks. Like the guerrillas. The road to hell is paved with good intentions. It turns his stomach to remember when he confessed and how his colleague embraced him, as if offering him redemption. It was a regrettable mistake. That little plaster saint, sooner or later, will shoot off his mouth. With the same naïveté he used to describe his Patagonian dream, tomorrow his colleague will blab about the clerk's family tragedy, his relationship with the secretary. Maybe he won't tell anyone in the office, but he *will* tell that little redhead. Let's suppose he tells his fiancée: exaggerating his intervention, he'll tell her about it. Little Red, as pure as he is, will feel like a big shot, too, when she hears the story because other people's misfortune always has the virtue of consoling us for our own. Since telling a story of suffering, in addition to producing a moral effect, makes a good impression and speaks well of the one who shares it, she, in turn, will tell a friend. This friend, amused by the story, will tell it to God-knows-whom. And just as they say that only seven people separate us from the King of England, his personal life, like a boomerang, will land in the office, and, like the completion of a perfect circle, will reach the boss's ears.

He has to wait, he tells himself. He'll think of some way to liquidate his colleague. He has to wait, just as now he's waiting for the secretary to come out of the boss's office. Waiting is not a passive state. It encompasses a series of actions that, although insignificant, undermine him. Loading the ink pad with ink, sharpening a pencil, or organizing the paperclips, can be very meaningful actions that stimulate reflection. The same as going over to the coffee machine, picking up a plastic cup, filling it, pouring in some sugar, stirring. Waiting is a deceptive peace.

Thoughts tumble around between his temples. His feeling of unease also consists of a stiffening of the back of his neck, a contraction of his jaw, pain in his back, and sweat that soaks his shirt collar. The first bats of the evening. He can hear them.

Maybe loneliness is the worst of all evils, he thinks. Maybe the boss feels lonely, he muses. The young woman feels lonely, too. His wife feels lonely. The litter feels lonely, and El Viejito, he recalls, El Viejito must be the loneliest of all. But their respective loneliness can't be compared to his. Returning home at the end of the day eats at his guts. A revelation interrupts him as he writes up a record, transfers a folder to another section. If the whole business with the secretary caused him such emotional upheaval, it was because he's afraid of being alone. But instead of making him feel less lonely, it made things worse. The loneliness the young woman injected into him is that of a desert island. Because the loneliness of a man in love is corrosive. Love has trapped him into a loneliness he wasn't used to, the loneliness of knowing that we're always alone. To envision that one might escape from oneself, be less like oneself and more like the Other joined with yet another, awakened an illusion in him. For a moment he believed he could be the Other. But his fear of abandonment has made him face the awareness of another kind of loneliness: the loneliness of loss. If it's true that you can only lose what you've never had, the loneliness of the man in love, a permanent awareness of that loss, gnaws at him.

He checks the time again. Those two are still in the office. He shuts his eyes. At this time of day, except for the lights on his desk and the secretary's desk, the office is suffused with an underwater light. He is a corpse that sinks to the bottom, among algae and schools of fish.

He bites the cuticle of his left ring finger; he pulls off a bit of skin with his teeth, hesitates between spitting it out or swallowing it, and finally he swallows it, thinking about the time he's wasted on all this activity, an action which, in its minuteness, frightens him. Why not go home right away, he wonders. Home, he says to himself. Sadly he thinks about the word *home*. However, he asks himself why not return home with a bouquet of flowers for his wife. After all, he consoles himself, if he gets sick, she, his wife, and no one else, will take his temperature, fix him some tea with lemon, remember to give him his medicine. Although it's also true: in these tender ministrations she displays more concern for his monthly salary than for his health. Marriage and family are a hideout. Everyone, all those men and women who want marriage, a family, seek nothing but a place to hide in and keep their most embarrassing secrets. And he wonders how his wife would react if he came home with flowers. It terrifies him to think it might turn her on. He can no longer recall the last time that, following her orders, he threw himself on top of her.

She doesn't caress him as much as rub him. Her gum disease disgusts him. She licks him, leaving spittle on his face. As his erection is slow, she puts his penis in her mouth. She swallows it. And then she lies on her back and hoists him on top of her, arranging him in position. He's grateful to be on top. If it were the other way around, their coitus would culminate in a fractured rib, a broken hip. She holds him by the waist, moving him up and down. He tries hard to keep his penis from going flaccid. He doesn't want to think what would happen if he got soft right now. He hears voices. It's time for the cleaners to arrive.

The motor of the vacuum cleaners. If the cleaning crew weren't here, he would lean against the office door, peek through the keyhole. Why imagine she's such a bitch, he asks himself. What's at stake in all his thoughts, he says to himself, is his courage. But to recognize his cowardice, he reflects, has its merit. To accept that one is a coward, he thinks, suggests a degree of honesty that other people aren't always prepared to tolerate. The coward who knows he's a coward, he deduces, has a kind of honesty that's lacking in someone who hurls himself blindly into battle to hide his fear. He's in the process of convincing himself of the logic of this argument when he thinks he hears someone whisper over his shoulder. It's the Other. A coward will always be a coward, the Other says.

He shakes his head in denial. He looks around. The only thing he needs now is for the cleaners to see him debating with himself. It's not in his best interest to contradict the Other, who always tries to make him look ridiculous. He's prepared to concede to the Other as long as he'll leave him in peace with the files and checks. It makes no sense to continue in this vein. But the Other, ironically, persists. He can't fool him. Nobody knows him like the Other. He was, is, and always will be witness to all of his humiliations.

A helicopter flies lower than usual. The noise of the engine is deafening. Its searchlights are blinding. The blades slice the bats into pieces. The engine, the blades, the searchlights, the frightened bats. One after another, the smashed bats are bloody shadows that crash against the windows. Magnetized by the helicopter, in a frenzy, their scattered pieces fly in the light of the choppers. And when one of them, decapitated, splats against the windows, it spurts a stream of blood. The bleeding bats crash against the glass. The way those nocturnal creatures flap their wings blindly, heading toward their own destruction, must be a sign. The suicidal bats make him dizzy.

29

LATER, JUST LIKE EVERY OTHER NIGHT OF HIS LIFE, he turns off the computer, stores his office supplies, puts on his jacket, takes his overcoat down from the coat rack. He checks the time. Enough. He's waited long enough. One more moment and he'll fall apart, he thinks. If she comes out of the office and finds him still here, she'll think he's a driveling idiot. It would be best for him to hurry, to depart once and for all. He's in the process of putting on his overcoat when she appears at the office door. Wait for me, she asks. The clerk's legs buckle.

Would he like to walk with her, she asks.

He smiles, spellbound.

After a few blocks, she takes him by the arm. As words and gestures tumble out one after another, everything seems like a dream come true. It pains him to think that what's tragic about a dream is that it can't become reality. That's called waking. Because once you develop a taste for the dream, life becomes intolerable if it doesn't happen again. And then you feel more miserable than before, when you didn't know that dreamlike happiness.

If only he could stop thinking, he says to himself. They walk along in the frigid, foggy night. They step around the last, straggling employees and the homeless, huddling in doorways and arcades, wrapped in their grimy, ragged blankets, in cardboard boxes where they take refuge from the polar temperatures. Some stake their posts beneath still-lit windows. Shop windows. Clothing. Furniture. Notions. Small appliances. Dishes. Tools. Jams and preserves. Cosmetics. Audio. Toys. Liquor. Pets. The clerk and the secretary look in a veterinary window containing pets: dogs, cats, rabbits, parrots, multicolored fish. Newly cloned, a sign promises. Two-year warranty.

Beneath the shop window, the homeless fight over a carton of wine, pushing, laughing. At first the battles are a pretense, then a genuine row. A woman socks a drunk. She takes his wine. The drunk comes back at her with a punch in the mouth. The woman lets go of the carton. It falls. The wine spills. Enraged, the guy kicks the woman. The others begin to cover themselves with their rags and cardboard boxes; they grumble. The guy stumbles closer to the group. By piling up on one another, they conserve heat for the night. A cold drizzle falls. It's colder than last night. Below zero.

He takes the young woman's hand. They walk by those who are lying down. An old woman, her face crossed with brown and black scabs, reaches out a dirty, wounded hand to beg. He pulls the young woman away. The beggar asks him if his little whore is so expensive that he doesn't even have a penny left for a poor old lady. The band of gargoyles laughs at her wit. The old woman heaves with laughter.

With the sprawling crowd behind them, he asks her what kinds of movies she likes. Comedies, the young woman replies. Romantic comedies. She recites her favorites. He likes comedies, too, he says. But he likes crime dramas better. Especially those where you know who's guilty from the beginning and you just have to wait for them to get caught. He wants to change the subject. Because if the young woman asks him to take her to the movies, he won't have enough money to buy the tickets and invite her out for pizza afterward. Moving the conversation in a different direction, he says that he loves people with a sense of humor who smile at adversity. Problems look different over time, he says. Time is like distance: the farther you get from a problem, the less intense it seems. Comedy, for example, is tragedy plus time. Her interest piqued, she says she didn't know he was a philosopher. He replies that we all carry a philosopher or an artist inside, but not all of us are lucky enough to express our talent, and that's true of him, after all his years working at an office, his responsibilities, obligations that he always wanted to get out of in order to develop a life more in accordance with his ideals, a fuller life. For example, he says, in Mozart's day a worker earned twenty-five florins a year. Mozart, on the other hand, earned more than a thousand florins per concerto. He would have liked to be a creator. She says that she would have liked to be an actress. But when she had the chance, she let it go by. She thought most actors starved to death. But she was misled. So she just had to learn to deal with it. Now she's a nobody, just the same. In life we all get an opportunity. If we let it go by, we're screwed. He shouldn't complain, she consoles him, because it's not so bad to be the boss's confidant, his right hand man. Just the mention of the boss puts him on alert. Why is she talking about the boss, he wonders. He never would have imagined that the boss valued him. He has to believe her, she says. She knows what she's talking about. Again, jealousy. He imagines the secretary and the boss; he imagines the two of them making fun of him. What could the boss have said, he wonders. Why is he suddenly so serious, the secretary asks. The fact that he's not an artist doesn't mean he isn't valuable as a person. She's right, he concedes. Going back to comedy, he says. If she enjoys comedy, he thinks, while they're together, instead of bitterly describing their respective problems, it would be good to do it with humor, looking forward. At least that's what he's been doing since the night they spent together, because ever since that night, his life changed. Today was a happy day, he says. His hands are damp as he says this. She walks along, deep in thought. She doesn't want to speak of love yet, she says. It's too soon.

Honestly, he thinks, the great existential dilemma is memory. It makes you unable to forget who you are, he says to himself. Because if he could forget himself, his hands wouldn't sweat. If only he didn't have a conscience. Conscience is like those helicopters that fly over the city, always looking for unrest. In spite of the helicopters' vigilance, he doesn't want to place too much trust in this wandering through the deserted streets. He'll have to figure out where to take the young woman pretty soon. If they go directly to her apartment, she might not invite him in tonight. He mustn't forget the hours she was holed up with the boss in his office. He can't, he mustn't, be too trustful. He needs to think. He needs to think of something soon. He needs to think really soon of a place to take the secretary to prolong their time together. Besides, in a little while the downtown streets will become a no-man's-land.

There are so many places he'd like to take her. But none of them is within his means. One, he says to himself. Surely there has to be one. Then he asks the secretary if she likes kids, and she answers yes. To have kids is one of her deepest, most personal desires, she confesses. Speaking of kids, he says, if she likes kids, she has to like kickboxing, those fights between youngsters. She reacts enthusiastically: she's crazy about kickboxing. She's gone to watch kickboxing a few times. She avoids mentioning whom she went with. One of these evenings, he promises, he'll take her to a kickboxing competition. At first the little champs were Filipinos, but with growing worldwide attention, in our city there's now a first line of fighters and a second one with kids from everywhere. Those fights are really something, she exclaims. The kids, no matter how small, are pure muscle. Their agility is incredible, the way they shine in the ring. Too bad such ferocity, like so many lovely things from childhood, gets lost when they grow up. The same courage that a fighter uses to kick his opponent's face in can be used by the other guy to bite off his ear and spit it at the audience. It's true that lots of kids fight without ever becoming champions and are left behind along the way, broken and brainless, useless for any other kind of activity, but no one will ever rob them of that lightning bolt that brought them glory, teaching the adults how you need to fight for your life. She isn't bothered by the blood, she says. If she had a son, she'd send him to kickboxing practice. The future looks uncertain for future generations. Training in management and fluency in several languages aren't enough these days. You've got to teach them a fighter's mentality. When she brings a new life into this world, she'll try to make sure it's been trained for the concrete jungle. She doesn't want her son to be a spineless wimp chained to an office job. Her offspring won't be some loser behind a desk, she says. She won't educate him to end up in a round of firings like these wretches, sleeping underneath a shop window, all lit up in the night for no buyers at all.

Her words pain him. He pulls his arm away. He lowers his head. She realizes she's hurt him. She stammers. She didn't mean to belittle him. She didn't mean to imply that he was a desk-bound loser. Who did she go to watch kickboxing with, he asks. And he understands that this is a question he shouldn't have asked. She looks at him. She looks at him in silence. She hesitates before replying. Ask me no questions and I'll tell you no lies, she says. It's late. She's tired.

He steps away. And she asks him what's wrong, what he's thinking about. She knows what he's thinking about. Fine, she says, annoyed: she'll tell him. She went to watch kickboxing with the boss, she says. They went twice, only twice, she explains. Well, three times, she corrects herself. It irritates her that he demands explanations. He's not asking her for explanations, he says. Curiosity, he says. Simple curiosity. And those times, in case he's interested, afterward they went to bed together. What else does he want to know. Does the boss satisfy her sexually, is that what he wants to know? If she loves the boss, is that what he wants to know, she asks. If he wants to know the details, he can go ahead and ask. Directly, he can ask her directly.

He's dying to know, but he won't ask. He apologizes: he didn't want to humiliate her. She's beside herself. He needs to get things straight, she says. She doesn't want to talk about love. She doesn't want to fall in love again. And it's too late to walk around downtown. She refuses to take a taxi. She thinks it's a waste of money. If they hurry, they can catch the last subway train. Suddenly she changes tone. She speaks to him like a little boy: he needs to be satisfied with what they have now. At her place there's some brandy left over from the other night. She smiles.

30

THEY TRAVEL ALONE IN THE LAST SEAT of the last subway car. The subway is dangerous at this time of night. The stations, deserted. At the next stop, a gang of skinheads with baseball bats might get on. The din of the train in the bowels of the city. Even though she's shouting, the young woman can barely be heard over the metallic clatter. She's careful not to mention the boss. Why doesn't she mention him, he wonders. He answers his own question—in order not to hurt him. Out of pity, he thinks. When she tires of shouting, he shouts out one of his typical sayings. The trip seems endless. Each time the train pulls into a station and the doors open, the clerk holds his breath until they close again. Sometimes, the two of them fall silent, their mouths dry. The sound of the steel encloses them in abrupt silences. Then they turn toward the window. He doesn't like to see her reflection because when she opens her mouth so wide, you can really notice her missing bicuspid. They have to shout to be understood. The effort deforms their faces.

The doors open and close at the stations. The ghost train seems lighter and swifter. He really should change his mood, he reproaches himself. Especially now that his dream is becoming a reality. As he slides closer to the young woman to hear what she's saying, a doubt gnaws at him. He wonders which of the two of them she might have fallen in love with, him or the Other.

They get off the train. The bang of the turnstiles. The echo of their footsteps. The only steps that can be heard in the tunnels. As they approach the escalators, the nighttime cold penetrates their bones. The apartment blocks aren't as close as he thought. They cross a concrete plaza. Here the night is blacker, the fog impenetrable, and the cold, biting. The closest residential building is a block away. If he were to kill the young woman, no one would hear a thing. Nobody, nothing. A perfect crime. One of many violent deaths in the area. In order to justify the crime, he would steal the money from her purse. The police would accuse some street kids. If he was found out, when the detectives interrogated him, he would reply that he killed her so as to remember her as beautiful forever. Where did he get this idea from, he wonders. Because he doesn't want the illusion to fade. She looks around. She's afraid, she says. He can't imagine how much violence there is in this area. She doesn't even feel safe in her own apartment. If someone broke into her apartment and attacked her, no neighbor would rush to help. Those who were awake, watching TV, would turn up the volume when they heard her screams. Those who were asleep, when the shrieks woke them, would roll over in bed and cover their heads with a pillow. Frightened by the silence surrounding them, she suggests they cross the street and walk on the opposite sidewalk, which is better lighted. Hurry, she says.

He can see the illuminated kiosk, the yellow light at the base of an apartment block. He can distinguish the silhouettes: boys and girls getting drunk. They hear the music. Calm down, he tells her. Not that she doesn't feel safe with him, but it would be best to take a detour behind a service station. He doesn't like the idea: the highway is only half a block away from the service station. And you don't know what you might find under its pillars. Summoning his courage, he tells her not to be afraid, to follow him, to walk confidently. Holding the young woman by the arm, he can withstand the terror. They approach the kiosk. The kids are dancing. Whatever happens, he has to keep going. He walks erect, holding her by one arm.

It takes them forever to get past the kiosk. They pass through the crowd of kids. Bodies, cheap perfume, sweat, booze. Dyed hair and shaved heads, tattoos and piercings. Combat gear and black jackets. They cross without looking to either side. They hear music, laughter, jokes. The music and frenzy of the gang. They're too drunk and strung out to notice the couple. He has trouble convincing himself that the worst is over.

They arrive at the apartment building. They enter the apartment, and she takes off her shoes. For him, it's as though she were taking off her clothes. Then she turns off her cell phone, lowers the volume on the answering machine, and disappears into the kitchen.

He studies each object again. Those plates on the walls, the porcelain figurines, family photos, framed diplomas, and teddy bears. So many teddy bears. Every item has a story, he thinks. And in every story there's a secret. He would like to reveal all his secrets.

She returns with two glasses, brings out the bottle of brandy. This woman knows what men want and what they can get in exchange, he thinks. She needed a drink, she says. He imitates her. The brandy burns. He wonders which of the two women is the real one: the one from the other night, or this one. He removes his overcoat and jacket, loosens his tie, takes another drink of brandy. Sitting on the sofa, with a feigned air of relaxation, he spreads his arms and stretches them over the backrest. He waits for her to sit down beside him. But she walks back and forth. She puts on music. A melancholic fox trot. Sadness weighs on his heart when she sits on a chair opposite him and crosses her legs on top of the coffee table. She laps up her drink. She looks at him suggestively over the rim of the glass. She asks if he masturbates.

He loves her, he replies. She says what she's said before: no love talk. Maybe he should go, he thinks. She touches herself. She asks him if he would masturbate for her. He doesn't masturbate. He'd rather make love, he says. He mustn't talk about love, she asks. Not tonight. Love is nothing but loneliness, she says. Please, would he touch himself for her, she pleads. If he'd like, she insinuates, she can help him. She comes toward him, unzips his fly, asks if he likes it. She touches herself, too. She tells him to watch how she touches herself. They touch themselves and look at each other. Her eyes fill with tears. He stops, looks for a tissue, but she asks him to go on. She cries and touches herself. Don't be distracted, she begs him. Go on, she asks. Don't stop. He's crying, too. But he likes it.

31

THREE A.M. ON ALL THE CLOCKS IN THE CITY. Three A.M. in the watery streets. Three A.M. in the doorways where the homeless lie. Three A.M. in the subway stations. Three A.M. in the concrete plazas. Three A.M. on the deserted highways. Three A.M. in the flaming embers of the last attack. Three A.M. in the guerrilla camp. Three A.M. in the barracks. Three A.M. on the airport runways. Three A.M. in the hangars, the helicopters now resting, their blades damp with bat blood. Three A.M. in the silent hospitals. Three A.M. in the police station cells and in the overcrowded jails. Three A.M. at the port. Three A.M. in the halls of government. Three A.M. in the abandoned office. Three A.M. in the apartment where his wife and the litter sleep. Three A.M. in the secretary's apartment. Three A.M. in the country house where the boss lives with his little Balkan adoptees. Three A.M. in the tiny apartment shared by the office mate and his fiancée. Three A.M. and he slides a fist into her vagina. The young woman pants, arches her back. On this early morning, at 3:00 A.M., he once more realizes that he can't live without her.

Even if she doesn't speak of love, he thinks she loves him. He thinks he understands her: she's afraid of another romantic letdown. Like with the boss. But, he figures, the boss must not have been as serious as he is. The boss must have impressed her with his social success. Dates, dinners, gifts. He, on the other hand, worked up the courage to tell the young woman all his feelings of shame. By offering his soul like that, he applied his strategy to win her over through pity. Exaggerating his sincerity, he gradually became a retouched photo of himself. The fact that she paid attention to him means that for the first time he's found someone to love him back. The secretary, on the other hand, hasn't shown him anything more than instant snapshots. But to him they seem like chapters of a novel. And he is her reader. Her great reader. Introducing a few fingers at first, then all of them, then his fist, and, once inside, opening his hand inside her, he thinks that in her fluid secretion, her voluptuous arching, she belongs to him as she's never belonged to anyone else.

But his torment doesn't dissipate. His jealousy remains. Every time she walks into the boss's office, he bites his nails, looks at the door, returns to a file, to the checks, and his eyes turn toward that door of their own accord. Sometimes he wonders what would happen if he dared to enter the office unexpectedly. What would he do, he wonders, if he surprised her sitting on top of the desk, her legs spread, clutching the boss's bald spot. If that were to happen, he concludes, he would step back timidly, apologize, close the door gently, and, as he left, determined to regain his composure, return to his desk, his heart about to burst. The files, the checks.

He spends several nights a week with her, but his pangs of jealousy don't go away. Isn't it possible that she spends the other nights with the boss? Isn't it possible that the young woman can work things out to keep two relationships going at the same time? With the boss, in exchange for a service, she's guaranteed concrete benefits. Her rent, for example. The boss must be paying her rent. And many other things. In the young woman's apartment, he's become an inspector. He investigates, looking for gifts. He investigates the bedroom, the closet, the drawers. He investigates in the living room, in her dresser. He investigates the bathroom, the medicine cabinet. He investigates in the kitchen. He looks for the boss's presence. There are times, when she's shaking with orgasm, that he wonders who could have taught her this caress or that one, one technique or another, this or that position, if it was the boss, if she likes the same things with the boss, or if she plays coy.

Early one morning, as he returns home, while his wife and the litter are asleep, he sprawls out on the sofa, turns on the TV, and channel surfs. He happens upon a quiz show. The contestant, a dwarf, locked in a booth with his heart connected to cables, grows uneasy. The cables, connected to a computer, control his heartbeats. Offstage, an announcer reads off a multiple choice question. A second hand starts to tick. The pulses mark the time. The more nervous the participant becomes, the more rapid the pulses, and these reduce the time he has to answer. The choices appear on a screen, and the ticks on a scoreboard. The question concerns sexuality and female anatomy. The dwarf is given different options to choose from to determine which scientist discovered the G-spot, so named for the first letter of his last name. The offstage announcer reads the names that appear on the screen: Greenwich, Grant, Goodman, González, Gutenberg, Ginsberg, Gutiérrez, Graffemberg, Goldenberg, Gómez. The dwarf faces a panel of buttons, and if he presses the correct one, the answer will light up and a triumphal fanfare of symphonic music will sound. If he makes a mistake, there will be a burst of laughter. The dwarf hesitates. On the audio monitor, amplified systolic and diastolic beats. The dwarf listens, deep in thought. The offstage announcer asks again, this time soberly, who discovered the G-spot. The dwarf's heart beats violently. His eyes pop out of their sockets. On tiptoe he reaches out toward the panel. He looks at the camera, frightened. He's about to press a button with his finger. But he holds back. Finally, with a little leap, he touches a button: Gutenberg. Laughter erupts on the audio feed, and the red-faced dwarf, grabbing his head, looks even more dwarfish.

What's the difference between him and that dwarf, the clerk asks himself. He turns off the TV and turns over, his face against the back of the sofa. How much longer can he put up with it, he wonders. The Other celebrates his despair. What you've got is guilt, the Other says to him.

Once more, the Other is right.

32

THE WOMAN WAKES HIM AND PULLS HIM OFF THE SOFA. She orders him to go directly to the bedroom and get undressed. He doesn't contradict her. He strips slowly. He covers his penis, his testicles. She rummages in a dresser drawer. A strap, some metal clips. She orders him to hurry and get in bed.

He's been acting very mysterious for a while now, the woman says. Maybe he's looking elsewhere for what he has at home. So many overtime hours and always returning at dawn makes a person think, she says. It's true that he's useless as a husband, and even worse as a father, but with so many catastrophes all around, there's a glut of merry widows in the city. Maybe one of them has stolen him away. It's better to open the umbrella before the rain comes. She ties him to the bars of the headboard. Don't be scared, she whispers. You're gonna like it.

Obese, coarse, it seems like he's seeing her for the first time. The fuzz beneath her nose. The hairs on her nipples and in her armpits. Her pubis is a jungle. He can smell the abundant sweat of her arousal. She clamps his nipples with the metal clips. He damn well better get an erection, she hints. She presses her vagina into his face, squashes it down on him, and brings his penis to her mouth. It feels like she's about to devour it. Practically suffocating, he separates the woman's buttocks and sucks her. She has a sour taste. When he finally achieves an erection, she pulls off her nightgown and inserts his penis into her. He's embarrassed that his erection lasts longer than any he's had with the young woman.

Afterward, smoking, she tells him that lately her desire has been rekindled. So tomorrow he'd better get home early. She definitely suspects something, he says to himself. Now the problem is what to say to the young woman. How will he explain that he won't be visiting her tonight, he wonders. It occurs to him to tell her that one of his kids, the weakest one, is sick. He's distressed as he talks to her about El Viejito. The young woman seems to believe him. When he returns home earlier than usual, his wife is waiting for him again. And the next day, at the office, he has to hide how battered he is.

That week he suffers a major gastric upset, with unbearable heartburn. Along with a constant headache. Not to mention the cramps, electric impulses that make his legs seize up. He's not as worried about a sudden cramp overtaking him at his desk as he is about getting one while having sex with the young woman. But worst of all is the sudden urge to urinate that's been affecting him lately. In the street, on the subway, in the boss's office, at lunch with the secretary. He has to dash off in search of a bathroom.

His trips to the bathroom don't go unnoticed by his office mate. One morning he approaches him, flashing that friendly little smile. Prostate? he inquires. I should cut back on the tea, he replies. The office mate looks at him: he hadn't realized he drank tea. You should be more observant, the clerk says. The office mate remarks: Drinking tea is so Russian.

Then he leaves his desk, goes to the bathroom, urinates, and, on emerging, walks into the boss's office. He needs to talk with him, he says. A confidential matter, he mumbles. He speaks in a low, nervous voice. His heart is beating like a drum. The boss leans back in his chair, asks him to calm down; if he has a problem that the boss can help solve, no worries. The boss holds him in the highest regard. The clerk's hands are cold, clammy. The highest regard, the boss repeats.

It's not about him, the clerk whispers. It's about his colleague.

33

THAT AFTERNOON, HIS COLLEAGUE IS LATE getting back from lunch. The clerk checks his pocket watch. A half hour goes by, one hour, two. The colleague doesn't return. And nobody seems to mind his absence. No one here is irreplaceable. The cemetery, if, in fact, his office mate is lucky enough to be buried in one during these times, is chock full of irreplaceables. The clerk goes over to the desk behind him, thumbs through a tray of files, pretends to look for one in particular, opens the desk drawer, and at last finds the notebook. Russian Notebook, his office mate has written on the cover. The clerk conceals the notebook in a file box and carries it over to his desk. Then he looks around. No one sees him as he hides the notebook. Or when he opens it and immerses himself in its pages. Contrary to what he had supposed, it's not a diary. Scattered notes. A few in Cyrillic. Notes on literature. If there was a chance that the notebook might help him discover some secret about his office mate, he's prepared to deal with it. Unless the secret is written in those hieroglyphics. He should have realized that the poor wretch had no secret more interesting than his pathetic literary dream of Patagonia. He was a poor, idealistic, pencil pusher. *Was*, he thinks. He's conjugating his colleague in the past tense. Which isn't exactly incorrect, he considers.

It's now after 7:00 P.M., the staff is leaving, and as usual, he'll stay behind till nighttime.

His office mate hasn't reappeared.

He never will again.

34

HIS COLLEAGUE'S ABSENCE IS STARTING TO BOTHER HIM. As day after day goes by, that absence saps his strength. Especially here, at work, where that absence, instead of scarring over, becomes infected. His thoughts are worms of guilt. He wouldn't be infected if he wasn't a rat. And if he acted like a rat, he tries to rationalize, he was forced into it by the circumstances. He wouldn't have denounced his office mate if the guy hadn't dragged a confession out of him. His office mate, with his sanctimonious tone, subtly pressed him into it. Because, as time goes on, every day he's more convinced that his colleague had it coming. And he also worked out a way to wheedle him into this guilt, an infectious guilt. The clerk swats at an imaginary fly. And a little later, another. He has to be careful to keep that gesture, which he makes when he's caught up in thoughts like these, from becoming a permanent tic. In the office they're going to take him for a madman, anyway. He wouldn't be the first to go crazy in an office like this, and he wouldn't be the last to throw himself out the windows, either. None of that's for him: neither first nor last, madman nor suicide. Maybe, he says to himself, the best thing for his mental health would be to take the bull by the horns. After turning the idea over in his mind, he's convinced he must see the girl.

He remembers the name of the gas station that he saw in the photo his office mate showed him. After consulting a guide to see which service stations are closest to the office, he makes a list of all of them, and visits them one by one on his lunch hour. He finds her in the last station on his list. The girl isn't smiling like in the photo. And, despite what his colleague told him, she's not smiling while waiting on customers. She must be embittered by his absence. Though it won't take her long to erase her memory of him by finding a replacement. Women are fast, he thinks. Faster than men. His time runs out; he returns to the office. He'll come back the next day, he vows to himself.

35

AND THE NEXT DAY, AT LUNCH HOUR, he sits down with a cup of coffee at the 24-hour bar. He can't deny that the bitterness lends the girl a sexy intensity. He changes his mind: maybe she's sexier now than before. He's attracted to her.

Every noon he sits at the service station bar. Same table, same tiny cup of coffee, next to the window. She moves around, indifferent to his spying. Until, in a single second, their eyes lock. She's discovered him. But she quickly feigns distraction. Just like his office mate when he would catch him writing in his notebook.

36

ONE AFTERNOON HE GETS THE IDEA TO ASK the boss's permission to leave early. Only rarely do employees ask to leave early. There has to be a very serious reason for someone to dare make such a request. And in his case, it's unprecedented. The boss is quite surprised that he, of all people, has come to ask him for this special permission. If something's going on with him, he should confide in him, the boss says. At first the clerk considers some excuse, an illness in the family. But it's an overworked story. If he invents something that resembles the truth, something he's about to do, he says to himself, it will seem more believable. He's got to risk it. The boss scrutinizes him with his gaze. What could he be up to, he wonders. The clerk hesitates and says he has an unavoidable commitment. The boss smiles. What kind of commitment, he asks. Could he be involved in some strange stuff? A date, he stammers. A date, the boss repeats. There is camaraderie in his expression. A skirt, eh? the boss asks, sounding him out. He lowers his head. The boss makes a joking remark. His date gambit really worked, he says to himself, his head still lowered. Because, incidentally, the boss will never suspect he's got something going on with the secretary. A date, he repeats. The boss laughs. Loudly. Who would've guessed, he says, roaring with laughter. Him, with his wimpy appearance, involved in chasing some skirt. The boss stands, places a hand on his shoulder. How could he refuse to grant permission when it comes to a little matter like that? With the dedication that the clerk shows at work, how could he deny him a bit of relaxation, the boss says. Besides, sticking your ass in the air has a secondary benefit. Because tomorrow you'll work twice as hard.

He moves fast as he leaves the office. He checks the time on his pocket watch. He walks quickly, almost running. He doesn't care if his limp is obvious.

Breathing hard, he arrives at the service station just as the girl is finishing her workday.

Without the uniform, without the gloves, in a black jacket, jeans, and sneakers, she's a different girl. A smaller one. Especially now that she's entering one of the oldest, most sordid neighborhoods in the city. Skyscrapers from the last century that became hives where destitution, sickness, and death pile up and multiply. Dark, narrow streets. Seedy bars. At every entryway a thug or a whore. Pestilential buildings that loom over the drunks and druggies. Every so often she steps over someone stretched out on the ground. Cloned dogs circle the bodies. Frequently a pack of dogs gets into it with the fallen, fighting them over a piece of meat. With the first light of day, a truck will come by and load on the scattered bodies. The collectors don't discriminate between someone who's unconscious or someone who's already gone to a better place. If they pick him up, when the unconscious man awakens, he'll find himself in a mass grave, licked by the crematory fire of the garbage dump. But it's still a while till morning. The clerk steps on glass as he walks: it's like stepping on needles. She plunges into the darkness. And reappears beneath some neon lights. She dodges a group of half-breeds, unperturbed. It's obvious that this neighborhood, where you can get your throat slit for a coin, doesn't frighten her. You need real balls to get lost in this neighborhood. But she doesn't get lost. She seems to know where she's going. Impossible not to compare her with the secretary. The little redhead is the anti-secretary.

At last she enters a bar. No one notices her. Those who aren't collapsed over a table sit rigidly in their seats. She sits at the bar. She lights a cigarette. She orders vodka.

He hesitates, not knowing whether or not to approach. There's an empty seat next to the girl. When the bartender asks him what he'll have, he orders the same thing she did. He's watched this scene in movies. All he has to do, he tells himself, is act.

She speaks without looking at him. Wasn't it enough that they picked her up and interrogated her at the police station, she asks him. How long were they planning to tail her, she demands.

I'm not an agent, he says. I'm a clerk, he tells her. A colleague of your fiancé. He found her by recalling a photo the colleague had shown him, a photo taken at the service station. His colleague had talked about her, about their Patagonian dream. That's how he found her. If he watched her without working up the nerve to start an honest conversation, he says, it was due to terror. Ever since his office mate's disappearance, he's been terrified. He has no doubt that his office mate was a man beyond suspicion, but at the office anybody can slander anybody else just to climb one rung higher. It could have happened to him. But there's more: after his office mate's disappearance, given how close together their desks were, now they might suspect him. It's true they haven't picked him up or interrogated him, but the way things are going, it could happen.

She finishes her vodka in a single gulp. She orders another. She knows who he is, she says. The Russian guy from the office. Her fiancé used to talk about him. He's so Russian, he used to tell her. So Russian. He appreciated him. She turns, observes him: You seem like a good man, she says. She's not suspicious anymore. She takes out her cell phone. She pushes some buttons and hands it to him. Listen, she asks.

The clerk recognizes his colleague's voice. He's speaking in a language that must be Russian. Yes, she says, it's Russian. He used to like leaving her little messages in Russian. And writing poems to her in Cyrillic. All she has left of him now is that voice on the cell phone. If only he had given her a child, she says, she'd have something to hold on to. But he didn't. She'll never have children. Not from someone else, either. Because after what they did to her at the interrogation she won't be able to have children. Not after that.

He's mute. He hasn't touched his glass. If he drinks, he'll lose control. He manages to take out the notebook and hands it to her. He explains that he rummaged around in his desk before they emptied it. And he salvaged this, the notebook. The notebook is what motivated him to look for her. Now it's hers. She doesn't have only his voice, he says. She also has his word. A word isn't a body, she replies. A word isn't a kiss. A word isn't a comfort. And neither is a voice on the cell phone. The girl doesn't cry.

Keep the notebook, she says.

He hesitates.

Goodbye, she says.

And she picks up the glass that he left untouched. She drinks the vodka as if it were water.

He's sorry he looked for her. He shouldn't have stuck his nose where it didn't belong. He'll walk out of her life just as he entered it, like a secondary character. He wonders how long he'll be a secondary character in everybody else's life.

Goodbye, he says.

And he leaves.

37

SOME TIME AGO HE STARTED BITING HIS NAILS. At first he thought it was a passing tic. But it turned into an obsession. In a science magazine he reads that the most evolved species use teeth and paws as weapons. Well then, he deduces, when he bites his nails, frightened by his pent-up violence, what he's really doing is eating his own aggression. One night as they lie in bed together, the secretary points out that he's biting his nails. He says that he does it to keep from scratching her while fisting.

Changing the subject, she says to him, he mustn't feel guilty. He puts on an astonished face. He doesn't know what she's referring to. Guilt, she replies, peering at him above her round glasses. Nail biting is a symptom of guilt. He still doesn't get it, he says. He shouldn't feel guilty for having ratted out his office mate. She, too, thought he seemed suspicious. He's about to ask her how she found out, but there's no need to reveal what he imagines: the boss told her. She confirms this, beating him to it: the boss told her, she says. And he should feel proud of what he's done. Because the boss will keep his loyalty in mind. She's proud of him, too, she tells him.

And now, she begs him, stop making that face and get on with the fisting.

Falling in love is a sickness. He's got secretary-itis. And if he does, he tells himself, this is the real key to explaining why he bites his nails. Now he understands why he had thought about killing her and immediately drove that fantasy from his mind. How can you love someone you fear, he wonders. Because, he realizes, she is possibly more frightening than the boss. But he doesn't have the courage to get rid of her, and he never will. And he doesn't have it because, as he knows, he couldn't live without her even if she were a cloned dog.

38

Sometimes he sneaks a magazine into the bathroom. Sitting on the toilet, he reads an article about a neuroscience conference. Studies of patients who have suffered localized damage in the frontal cortex area and who present serious deficits of pride, shame, and repentance. Others present difficulties in admitting intentionality. The conference also discussed empathy and morals associated with group behavior. Empathy moves us to act: seeing a person suffer in a given situation can cause us pain and activate the brain circuits connected with danger. A good example of this, the article says, is what happens in a nursery with a baby no more than 18 hours old. If the baby cries, the others also start to cry.

This example moves him.

39

ONE NIGHT HE INVITES THE YOUNG WOMAN to a kickboxing competition. The combatants in the preliminary fights are under fourteen years old and come from the poorest areas of the city. The matches are always bloody. Tonight, the last fight is for the South American championship, so the public is inflamed, waiting for butchery. The stadium boils, roars. They elbow their way through the crowd. Their stalls are just a few meters from the ring.

First to arrive at the ring is the challenger, a Criollo kid with a broken nasal septum, a wild expression, white shorts. He climbs up accompanied by his trainer and assistants, all of them boys. One look at the Criollo kid throwing punches and kicks into the air is enough to know that it wouldn't be a good idea to run into him in a dead-end street. Then, making his way among the throng, in red shorts, is the challenger, a Korean kid with a fierce smile, no less threatening than his rival. The bell rings.

They check each other out for a few seconds. They don't hesitate to attack. The Korean kid seems unbeatable, at least in the first exchange of blows. Every kick he throws hits the Criollo kid right in the face. Soon the Criollo has to step back, wipe the blood from his eyes, and take his distance, prepare his defense, create a counter-offensive. But the Korean kid doesn't let him recover. The Criollo kid, against the ropes, scuffles with the champ. No sooner does the referee separate them, than the Criollo jumps on top of his opponent. The Korean boy is caught off-guard by his adversary's reaction. The Criollo boy kicks, hitting one of the Korean's cheekbones. The audience jumps up and down, egging them on.

The young woman isn't shy about joining the ovations. Sometimes she cheers for one, sometimes for the other. Her admiration varies according to which one displays more power. She doesn't root for either one: all she wants is to see blood. One round follows another. In these contests the fighters earn points for destroying their rivals. There are no rules forbidding dirty tricks. The fight lasts until one of the contenders falls unconscious in a pool of blood. The young woman screams her head off. She curses at the Criollo boy with his bloody face, blinded, unable to locate his rival, who's enjoying it all, taking his time, and who finally delivers a flying kick that knocks him off his feet. When the Criollo kid falls, the Korean boy kicks him in the kidneys. The ref separates them. He starts the count. The Criollo stands up and attacks again. The two kids hit one another. Neither gives up. When one falls, the other laughs as he kicks him. Now the fallen one is the Korean boy. He crawls around in a stupor. The Criollo kid raises his arms and jumps around in a victory dance while the ref begins the count again.

But the Korean boy manages to get up and leaps, all-or-nothing, back into the fray. He adds a dramatic turn to the fight. He surprises his rival, but surprises the audience even more. The stadium seems to come tumbling down amid boos, applause, and whistling. The young woman screams, beside herself. Her cries are orgasms. She must be so wet, he thinks. He wonders how to connect that little girl in the First Communion photo with this out-of-control female who screams as the Korean boy hammers the Criollo's head.

As they leave the stadium, the young woman shuts down. Her silence, her coldness, drive him to despair. He recalls the remark she made on the second night: that if she brought a baby into this world, she would do everything in her power to train him to fight for his life and never to be a loser behind a desk.

He asks the young woman if she's feeling all right. She replies that she needs to return to her apartment, to be alone and think. He offers to come with her. She refuses. It's late, he says. He's not about to leave her alone. She replies that she's always managed on her own. That it would be best if they said their goodbyes right here tonight. What's wrong, he insists.

She's pregnant, she says. That's what's wrong. Now that he knows, could he please leave her alone. If that's her problem, he says, he can be part of the solution. She turns her back on him. She orders him not to follow her. She starts running away, breaks a heel, stumbles. And continues on her way, limping. Seeing her limp, he thinks they were made for each other. He can't decide whether to follow her or stay behind. She disappears into the mouth of the subway. He watches. He's alone on the avenue. From high up above the buildings, he's illuminated by the searchlight of a helicopter.

40

SOME TIME AGO, ART HISTORIANS WERE INVESTIGATING exactly
when Vincent van Gogh might have painted his *Evening Landscape
with Rising Moon*. It was known that the canvas had been painted
in 1889, but not the exact moment of its creation. By tracing Van
Gogh's correspondence with his brother Theo and his friend Paul
Gauguin, the historians estimated that the artist had painted the
work in the month of May, shortly after cutting off his ear and vol-
untarily admitting himself to the Saint-Rémy-de-Provence Sanatorium, in the south of France. From there, from the sanatorium,
Vincent had viewed the landscape. And in September, his brother
Theo received the canvas.

The clerk reads this story in one of his science magazines.
The incident fascinates him so much that as he reads it, he almost
misses his station. A group of researchers from the University of
Southwest Texas, the magazine says, was determined to solve the
mystery of the date of *Evening Landscape with Rising Moon*. With the
aid of astronomical calculations, topographical maps, aerial photo-
graphs, climate measurements, and a modicum of common sense,
the researchers traveled to the south of France, where they identi-
fied the landscape in the painting. After calculating the position of
Earth's natural satellite with astronomical software, they came up
with two possible days when the full moon would have appeared
above the horizon, just as Vincent had painted it. As in the painting,
the stalk of golden wheat now revealed itself to the investigators.
They concluded that the exact date of the painting was July 13, 1899,
at 21:08 hours. But what interested them the most and also interests
the clerk is that in less than a month the moon will return to the
same position that had inspired Vincent in the south of France.

He closes his eyes. He remembers his first night with the young
woman. If the entire solar system could replicate the Earth's rota-
tion, time, and space at his will, he says to himself, then he would

become the Other. And speaking of the Other, he thinks, we are all Others. He's more and more convinced that the secretary is also the Other: by day, a cordial professional; by night, the lithe little female who gets off by sticking a pink vibrator into his ass. He falls face first among the teddy bears she's piled up on the sofa. Who is he to judge the young woman. It would make more sense to examine his own behavior, he tells himself. Who does he think he is, he wonders over and over again. Nobody is just one type of person, he assures himself. Now he smiles and nods; tears well up in his eyes, clouding the shapes of the teddy bears.

As he reacts to this vision, he wonders how it's possible for her to ignore him, to avoid him, to not talk to him. Nevertheless, he leaves a message on her answering machine. He's prepared to take responsibility if he's the father, he says. He'll happily assume paternity, he adds. Because ever since he fell in love with her, he has become the Other. And if he's the Other, that child will be the Other's child. A boy, surely. A kickboxing champion, he says in his message on the answering machine. At the office, he approaches her, asking in a whisper if he is the father. Even if he isn't, he's willing to give the baby his surname. He doesn't care if it's the boss's child. He'll love it anyway. After all, he tells her, the boss isn't a bad guy. The boss has his problems, he says. And he asks her if she knows that the boss's kids are adopted. She doesn't even look at him. He needs to mind his own business, she says. But he wants to know, the clerk tells her. He needs to know.

41

HE CAN'T COME TO GRIPS WITH THE FANTASY of killing her. Everything that's been happening to him lately is her fault. If he hadn't fallen in love with the secretary, his office mate wouldn't have disappeared, the redhead wouldn't have been tortured, and the two lovers would have gone on with their dream of populating Patagonia. It's not that he doesn't have the desire to kill the secretary. But he thinks her death would also mean the death of a new life that might possibly change both of their lives. This is what he thinks every time he imagines himself strangling the young woman. His hands close around her neck. She struggles for breath; her skin turns purple. She scratches him. She tries to scratch his eyes out, but he doesn't release the pressure till her body stops moving. What torments him most are the corpse's open eyes. He knows that that expression, like memory, will pursue him, follow him wherever he goes, no matter where he hides.

As if that weren't enough, lately he's started to have a scalp problem: dandruff and hair loss.

The dandruff and hair loss torment him. That's life, he reflects: in the middle of a drama, a minor inconvenience comes along and distracts us. And this secondary misfortune takes on major proportions. The Other is reflected in a pharmacy window; he walks into the store and inquires about scalp medications, tonics, lotions, and also the prices. The most effective remedies are the most expensive. The Other doesn't worry about price or about how the expense will affect his budget. His only concern is the scalp problem. He doesn't want to go bald like the boss.

The Other will decide for him. With decisive courage the Other works out a plan. Every day he hands over the checks to the boss and waits until he signs them. Sometimes the boss signs them while he's talking on the phone. It's not always the same scrawl. But he has studied all its variations. He can imitate him so no one notices the difference between the original and a forgery. With a check and a briefcase, he'll head for the bank, pocket the cash. Then he'll walk into a travel agency. This is the plan. A simple plan.

Tonight he returns home early. His wife and litter are sleeping. He closes all the windows and turns on the gas. It grieves him to kill El Viejito. He stops for a moment, watches him sleep, adjusts his blanket. El Viejito looks so much like him. But he can't take him along; El Viejito would be a burden. He needs to travel light. His guilt is heavy enough. The Other convinces him—you don't get very far with pity.

The next morning, the helicopters appear to be flying lower. Raising his eyes, he can make out the cannons on the machines, poised to shoot. Even though explosions are routine, he must take precautions. He can't let a nearby attack ruin the plan. Maybe it would be a good idea to take a taxi. But he runs the risk of getting stuck in traffic.

He enters the bank. A teller with a visor examines the check. It's a significant sum. He needs to speak to the manager. Seconds become minutes. The Other remains calm. At last the manager beckons him. They pass through a corridor, doors with iron bars. At the end of the hall stands an armed guard. The manager issues an order. The last gated door opens. A gigantic safe.

Minutes later, with his briefcase full of bills, he walks into a travel agency. A saleswoman offers him different vacation packages. He listens, thumbs through brochures. He'll buy a ticket in the secretary's name. A ticket to Mexico. She'll wait for him in Mexico. Meanwhile, he'll travel overland: a bus to the Brazilian border. In Brazil, another bus, this one to São Paulo. Then another to Rio. He'll change cities often. He'll cross the Amazon, and then, heading north along the Pacific coast, he'll catch up with the young woman.

Next to my bed I will place your nest
Where you can watch the days go by

[103]

For I, like you, have lost my way
And, O holy Heaven,
I cannot fly.

A straw hat, sunglasses, a black mustache, a brightly-colored shirt, white pants and shoes, with the briefcase always in his hand, beneath a scorching sun, he walks along a deserted street at siesta time. The song comes from a cantina. There are a few locals sprawled over the tables. In one corner a dark-haired girl with braids plays the guitar. Between the strum of one chord and another, in the silence, flies are buzzing.

He orders mezcal. He looks around. He doesn't need the money anymore. In order to get here, he realizes, he didn't need to do all he did. He didn't need to become desperately, passionately involved with the young woman, ending in a pregnancy. He didn't need to snuff out the lives of his wife and children in the name of that passion. And he didn't need to steal. As he recalls each of these acts, he feels tired. He wonders if everything he did for happiness' sake didn't lead to too much unhappiness. Now he realizes that happiness isn't what he thought it would be. Maybe happiness consists of the desire to be happy. This table, this girl, the song of the swallow. Now all he cares about is the cool breeze in the cantina, the mezcal, the song. He yanks off his fake mustache. Rubbing his hand across his forehead, he notices that his sweat is tinted by the hair dye. He takes off his glasses. He realizes that destiny had been saving a message for him. The message is in the bottle. And the message is a worm.

He polishes off the mezcal and swallows the worm. The worm of guilt. The girl stops singing. He walks over to her. He no longer tries to hide his limp. He hands her the briefcase. Then he leaves.

Once more in the glare of the sun. All he wanted, he says to himself, was to be someone else—the Other. But he's not the Other; he's the same as always, numbly sitting in an empty subway car in the dark, awakening from a dream, nodding with fatigue, with a pasty mouth and the nausea of having swallowed a worm. Now, waking up in the darkness, his heart pounding, he understands: he fell asleep on the last subway and he's alone at the end of the line, passing the last station, the terminal, in a labyrinth of tunnels and rails where the trains will remain motionless until tomorrow. He's trapped. He has no choice: he will spend the night here, on the halted subway in this labyrinth.

He doesn't even have any light by which to read this science magazine. His feet are frozen. He trembles. He sneezes.

42

Not even when there's a downpour, like tonight, do the helicopters stop flying over the buildings. The rain pelts the office windows.

He can't bear being at the office. Lightning illuminates the coffin-like desks. He stares at the one behind his. Every so often he opens the notebook. He reads a few lines. And then he places it back in the drawer. The desk has remained empty since his office mate disappeared. If he hasn't been replaced, the clerk thinks, there must be an explanation for the empty space. On the one hand, he reasons, the void might be a sign that the higher-ups are cutting costs, and it wouldn't be surprising if, when least expected, there's another purge of personnel. On the other hand, that absence has become a nearly tangible mass and a punishment: since his office mate's disappearance, he thinks of him more and more often, and sometimes—though no one but he can see—he observes him as he did when he was alive. Then he spins his chair around suddenly and, instead of his colleague, the Other is there, writing in the notebook. He's sorry he can't get rid of the Other, just as he did with his office mate. Because in order to get rid of the Other, he first needs to get rid of himself.

There's another possibility, he thinks. The empty desk might be a permanent sign of the boss's power, one of his Machiavellian tricks, in this case applied exclusively to him as a reminder that he's a snitch. And everybody knows a snitch is lower than someone who says no, as his office mate tried to do with his little rural dream. This alternative contradicts what the secretary told him, that the boss has held a higher opinion of him since he denounced his colleague. Now he's completely convinced: the boss will not replace the colleague behind him until he, tormented by his own vileness, ends up throwing himself out the window, falling into the night, and dying in a splattered heap. He imagines himself seen from up here:

a clot down below. More than one man, more than one woman, has committed suicide by jumping out the windows. Like bats, they too were chopped into pieces by the helicopter blades.

He walks over to the coat rack, puts on his overcoat. He doesn't even care about the pathetic state of his coat anymore.

Her pregnancy doesn't show yet. It's true that it's very recent. But she might also just be late. A false alarm. Could it be a trick, he wonders. She hasn't spoken to him since the kickboxing night. Every night he wanders aimlessly, going around and around, losing his way, always erratically, taking his chances with the cloned dogs, bomb fragments, crossfire, roundups, or the police, who could pick him up as a suspect. Leaving the office, he starts meandering around. The cold and damp, fatigue, and leg cramps make his limp more obvious. He's in no hurry to get home. There are nights when he sees himself reflected in shop windows, and the Other, from the reflection, casts him an ironic glance.

It's pouring when he goes out into the street. The wind turns every cloudburst into a waterfall. He crosses through a blare of honking horns. He's soaked. Darkness. The violence of the storm has caused blackouts in several sections of the city. The thunder and lightning blend with the din of a bomb exploding on the next block, on the top floor of an embassy. The traffic lights aren't working. Cars and buses get stuck. Whenever there's a storm of this magnitude, as the night progresses, entire areas of the city go dark. All the homeless people in the city go on the rampage, looting and killing. If he wants to get home, he'll have to escape. Now or never. Many employees opt to leave early or stay over at the office. It's safer to work all night without sleeping than to risk the predators who hold you up on the streets and avenues, just for the sake of a few hours of sleep in your own bed. The police and the military patrol indiscriminately. After a stormy night like this, piles of corpses show up at daybreak: men, women, old folks, kids. The madness makes no exceptions. But he's not in any hurry to return to his apartment. He makes it over to the opposite sidewalk, soaked to the skin, and takes shelter in a doorway. From here he can see the entrance to the building where he works. He wants to find out if, as in the dream, she'll leave in the boss's car.

She comes out of the building. Through the main entrance, hurrying and alone, she comes out. She notices him spying on her, following her. She walks along nervously. She stops at the entrance to the subway. It's closed, a sign that service has been interrupted. She crosses an avenue, dodging cars and trucks, armored cars and motorcycles, ambulances and patrol cars. She escapes. He follows her. Thanks to his limp, he stumbles. The tide of vehicles surrounds him. Sheets of water from the passing traffic whip his face. Soon, when the young woman realizes that she has no way to get back to her apartment, when every avenue is a battleground, every corner an ambush, desperate, she'll have to accept his company.

Her silhouette grows blurry in the deluge. She turns onto a dead-end street. His limp keeps him from running faster. He slips. She enters the dead-end street. A black hole. The darkness frightens him. Also the stench in the air. He cautiously takes one step, then another. He disappears into the cul-de-sac. Dumpsters, boxes, garbage cans. On this street the rain echoes louder.

The blow strikes him in the back, knocks him down. He loses his vision. When he opens his eyes, he finds himself lying in a puddle. The secretary stands in front of him. She has a weapon. She holds it in both hands. She mustn't over-exert herself, he tells her. Not in her condition; it isn't good. She raises the weapon. He moves away in time. The gun strikes the concrete. He lifts his arms, expecting another blow. He can't avoid it.

After the rain comes an impenetrable drizzle. When he regains consciousness, leaning against a wall, he exits the cul-de-sac. There is less traffic on the avenue. Military carriers are stationed on one corner. He tries to act self-confident. He heads for the other corner.

Again his usual nightly route. He sees human outlines and hears shouts. Every so often a flash explodes nearby. A scream of pain. Someone falls.

When he finally awakens, he doesn't know how he got home. He's lying on the floor face-up. The litter gathers around him, looking at him as if he's an insect in its death throes. They drool as they gaze at him. Somebody prods him with their toe to see if he's still alive. The woman shoos the litter away. She lines the fatties up and sends them off to school. Then she sees to his needs. She pulls him by one arm, flings him over her shoulder, and carries him to the bathroom. She puts him under the scalding shower. She administers a few blasts of cold water. Swallow the aspirins, she orders. And finish the black coffee. The woman cleans his pants, his suit, his overcoat. As he waits, sitting in a chair in his underwear with the cup of coffee, she irons his clothing. She scolds him and threatens him with the iron.

43

THIS MORNING HE'S A ROBOT who goes around with a power failure. He wears the contorted face of someone who has slept badly and shaved worse. Comments, laughter. Everyone looks at him; everyone knows his days are numbered. The murmur of voices is a shadow that reaches his desk. The young woman remains indifferent. He makes do with the pain of absence, the only aspect of the young woman he still clings to. The pain guarantees her memory in his body.

Then night comes again. He wanders the streets, walking endlessly. It's cold. The wind whips through an intermittent drizzle. But he doesn't stop. Walking keeps him warm. He moves his lips, muttering. But he's not talking to himself. He's arguing with the Other. He lowers his head, shakes it vehemently. He's against everything the Other says to him. The Other is responsible for all his misfortune. He'd like to get rid of him. But he doesn't know how. He's approaching the port when he has an idea: the way to get rid of the Other is by throwing himself into the water with a paving stone tied around his neck. By drowning himself, he will also drown the Other. It's a good idea, but there's one problem: he doesn't want to die yet. The idea, he realizes, comes from the Other, who wants to get rid of *him*. The Other has thought about killing him, but he won't give him the satisfaction. He might be mediocre, but he's no idiot.

This section of the port has become a fashionable spot. The docks were recycled, the piers converted into moorings. Sailboats, launches, yachts. Imported cars, convertibles and limos, screech to a halt and take off again, enveloped in the lights of restaurants, bars, nightclubs, and discos. The neon lights are shaped like galleys and canes, dice, high-heeled shoes, poker cards, red lips. Each place, each club, leaves its doors ajar; party music filters out. Laughter, champagne corks popping, echoes of dancing. Valets, thugs in suits, chauffeurs who look like gunmen, bodyguards stationed at the doors—all of them are elegant apes. Somebody laughs at him. It's the Other. He starts arguing with the Other again.

A young blonde emerges from a club. Her half-open fur coat reveals an ultra-tight black minidress with a plunging neckline, all decorated with crystals. She laughs, hanging on the arm of a graying fat man in a tuxedo who could easily be her father. Or her grandfather. The couple waits for a car to pull up. A luxury car with a chauffeur, he thinks. The tuxedoed old guy lights a cigar. The young woman's coat gapes open. He can see her toying absent-mindedly with a jeweled necklace. He wonders what it could possibly be worth.

According to the Other, with that jewel he'd be able to solve quite a few problems. Quite a few, he repeats. A salary would never be enough to pay for those stones. He could settle all the debts he owes with those stones. The secretary would regard him differently if he gave her even one. Just one of those stones. But he doesn't want to listen. If he had the nerve, the Other insists, he could grab that treasure. All he'd have to do is walk over to the young woman, smack the old guy in the tuxedo, grab the necklace and disappear quickly into the fog. He's tired of listening to the Other. Now the Other will see who he is, he thinks. The old guy chews on his cigar. The young woman hangs on his arm with a girlish giggle.

He picks up momentum, bumps into the old guy, knocks him down. The young woman is startled. He pulls on her necklace. A few stones fall off, but he runs away with those he's able to snatch. The old man, cursing. He runs. The girl, shrieking. He runs. A whistle. He runs. If he turns around he's done for. He runs. He feels a sharp pain in his chest. He runs. He can't catch his breath. He runs. A cramp in one leg. He runs. Halt, someone shouts. He runs. A gunshot in the night. He runs. Another gunshot. He runs. The lead rebounds, a nearby tinkling. He runs. A guard intercepts him. The guard knocks him over. He hits him in the head with the barrel of his gun. The clerk falls, face first, onto the pavement. They cuff his hands behind him. The guards' shiny shoes. Little sparkles on the wet sidewalk, the stones from the necklace. His nose itches but he can't scratch it.

He thinks about what the people at the office will say, he thinks about the young woman, he thinks about his wife, he thinks about the litter, he thinks about El Viejito. He reproaches himself for always thinking of El Viejito last. He imagines a cell at the police station, the prisoners looking at him out of the corner of their eyes. Police sirens. Tires screeching. Patrol car doors opening and closing. Black leather boots. A kick to the kidneys. He feels like throwing up. They pick him up by his hair, bend him over the car's engine, frisk him, take his papers, the light of a flashlight, and using the patrol car's radio, they check to see if he has a record. He doesn't. The cops mention something about a judge. It takes him a while to figure out who they're talking about. They're talking about the old guy in the tuxedo. The old guy is a judge.

They interrogate him. Where he lives, what he does. He answers, on the verge of tears. Keep a shred of dignity, he admonishes himself. The Other, watching him from behind the police, flashes him an ironic glance.

A black limo pulls up. One of the car windows is lowered, and then the clerk can just barely make out the judge and his little lady friend. Your Excellency, they call the judge. The clerk begs for forgiveness. Your Excellency, he snivels. It's the first time, he says. He did it out of need. He has so many mouths to feed, he explains. Please have pity, he sobs. Your Excellency, he says, kneeling. A cop smacks him in the face. But he doesn't stop beseeching.

The judge nods. The limo takes off into the mist. And they set him free. It's just wasn't worth it, the cops laugh. The stones were worth nothing. It's not that the judge was benevolent. It's that the necklace was a cheap fake. You were lucky, the cop tells him. It wasn't worth the effort of making a scene over some trinket given to a lady of the night.

44

HE READ AN ARTICLE IN A SCIENCE MAGAZINE about an experiment that was carried out at an institute of cognitive neuroscience. The experiment focused on a form of dementia that can erupt unexpectedly and lasts approximately seven minutes. But, the psychiatrists emphasized, there have been some cases in which the patients, even when they recovered from the shock of those seven minutes, seduced by their effect, repeated the actions they had carried out during the attack. Prudent men who became compulsive gamblers. Top-notch executives who one morning, on getting up to go to work, jumped off the balcony of their penthouse. Soldiers who, during a confrontation with guerrilla fighters, turned around and machine-gunned their own comrades. Housewives who unexpectedly abandoned their homes and took to the road in search of emotional experiences. Surgeons who, in the middle of an operation, stabbed their patients with the scalpel. Airplane pilots who, with a smile on their faces, decided to crash into the ocean along with the entire crew. In short, spirits that, in a burst of inspiration, took a path of no return.

The research project offered a wide range of examples, each of them more outrageous than the last. That article damaged him. He wondered if his falling in love might have been the result of this unanticipated madness. His attempt to steal a piece of jewelry was a clear sign that he's capable of losing his reason. The Other walks guardedly beside him. And nods. It's true that all love contains some measure of dementia, he says to the Other, but what he feels now responds to a certain logic. All his life he's dreamed of someday having a romantic adventure that would turn his existence around, lending it a touch of wildness. The problem, he now tells himself, is that falling in love didn't lead him to the path of no return. There's no difference between him and a common adulterer. None, he thinks.

Insecurity consumes him. He wonders if he should test the resistance of his love. Why not, he thinks. And now, when the subway stops at the station of his sin, he gets off. In fact, the station is named for a holy virgin who, among her many other powers, is believed to restore purity to those who have lost it.

Determined to put an end to his doubts, he climbs up to street level and finds himself in the red-light district. Unlike other parts of the city, this neighborhood never sleeps. Just as on these streets you can't tell if it's night or day, neither does anyone pay much attention to the kind of people who come here in search of a moment's pleasure. Here you're as likely to see an expensive convertible cruising slowly down the street as a grandmother ready to exchange currency for a reasonable fee. Male and female whores, kids, sell their bodies as well as drugs. Think of a drug, no matter how destructive, and you'll find it here. Imagine a pleasure, no matter how outrageous, and here it is, within the consumer's grasp. The clerk once read that man's imagination is limited when it comes to monsters. In a way that's what consumers like these youngsters are. But they feel like users, not monsters. Those who come here as customers know what they want. And the kids sell it and know how to charge for it. Prices vary, for basic coitus, for the immediate relief of a blow job, for pleasures that might include a partial mutilation or even death. The arrangement is always made with an older kid who might be a brother, a cousin, a father, with whom the erotic game and its price are agreed upon. In the event the client is interested in an erotic game that will put the child's life in danger or require his death, a special price is determined and a form filled out indicating the beneficiaries of the child's insurance policy.

He walks into the heart of the red-light district, though it's not his first time: he's walked these streets before in fits of anguish, but always without the nerve to request a service, out of fear of contracting a plague. He watches the boys and girls and can't stop thinking about El Viejito. He mustn't think about El Viejito now. He ought to think about this young girl who's offering herself to him. She can't even be six years old, but in her smile you can imagine everything you might do with that little, crimson-petaled mouth. He resists the temptation. He continues on his way. He crosses paths with a boy, In fact, he can't determine if it's a boy or a girl. A beautiful example of an androgynous little male. Or little female. As he thinks of these diminutives, he wonders why diminutives are the patrimony of childhood. He also wonders if these children, like the legless one who passes him by on a board with rollers, are not so much children as products. He thinks: if those who come to these streets to take their pleasure are consumers, the children—let's forget about scruples here—are products. And none of this, he says to himself, has to do with love.

Because one of the characteristics of love consists of feeling like a child. A child isn't a madman. He's simply not responsible for his actions. Neither he nor the secretary are responsible for the magnetism that brought them together. They're like children. Helpless against an all-powerful force that swept them up like a tornado. They didn't choose to fall in love. It happened to them. To him, at least. In his case, love is outside his area of responsibility. Neither a consumer nor a product, he says to himself. A child, he thinks. Suddenly he feels ashamed of walking these streets.

The thought of someone discovering him around here throws him into a state of panic. Someone who later will announce at the office that they surprised him wandering around this part of the city. It makes his heart race to imagine what the secretary might think when they come to her with this tale. He rushes toward the subway. But he's halted by the wailing of police sirens, the squealing of police car tires, patrol cars screeching suddenly to a halt, orders shouted by the police, their weapons aimed at him. He raises his hands. All around him everyone runs, adults and children alike, and he stands there alone, on the sidewalk outside a porn shop.

He raises his hands. He shouts that he hasn't done anything wrong. That he was just passing through. That he's not one of those degenerates who frequent the shop. But the police keep their weapons aimed at him. And then he notices that someone is poking cold metal into the back of his head. Behind him, shielding himself with the clerk's body, is a kid armed with an automatic pistol. He tries to turn around, but the kid, a bleached-blond mestizo, shakes him by the neck, hits him with the weapon. The pistol looks like an enormous toy. The kid sticks the weapon against his head again. The clerk's legs tremble.

Before, in his previous life—and when he thinks of his previous life, he thinks about the time before he fell in love with the secretary—many nights he wandered around, trying to delay going home, if home is what you call a hole like that. He enjoyed meandering along the downtown streets and continuing on to the edge of town, taking greater risks, imagining his bravery if someone managed to assault him. Once, a transvestite cornered him. When the clerk told him he wasn't looking for sex, the other guy slapped him in the face, took his money, and hit him again before leaving him, battered, in a doorway. Another time, several of them accosted him. They smacked him around, squeezed his testicles. And in the tangle of bodies shaking him, one of them swiped his wallet. The worst part wasn't losing a few bills. The worst part was losing his ID. If he reported it, he thought, if he declared that he had been mugged by transvestites, the police would doubt his own virility. He made up a lie. A kid, he lied. The kid had pointed a weapon at him. And his blood pressure dropped; he fainted. He couldn't recall anything else. When he became aware of his surroundings, he was wandering, lost. The shock prevented him from remembering more. That's what he declared in the guardhouse. All he cared about was getting his ID back.

45

THE TREMBLING IN HIS LEGS. They buckle beneath him. He can barely remain upright. His teeth chatter. His mouth has gone dry.

The police, in front of him, take aim. Grabbing him by one arm, the kid orders him to walk backward slowly. As the clerk and the kid retreat, the police advance. The kid laughs. He's amused by the situation. Kill or die, the kid says. And he laughs. That's what life is all about, the clerk thinks. Kill or die. He's always known it. It's hard for him to believe that the kid has summed up a philosophy of life so simply. He must be an angel who's come down from heaven to bring him this message. An emissary, he thinks. Maybe El Viejito was also an emissary and the bearer of a message that, at the time, he was unable to understand.

46

HE DOESN'T KNOW HOW LONG HE'S BEEN LIKE THIS, his legs buckling, his teeth chattering, his mouth dry, his armpits soaked, his hands in the air. And the urge to urinate. He's been this way his whole life, he thinks. He thinks that ever since he's had the capacity to remember, he's found himself with the barrel of a gun at the back of his head. He can't take it anymore.

As he loses consciousness, as he collapses, he feels lighter than a pillow. He surrenders to the blackness. In the distance, gunshots sound.

47

HE'S SITTING ON THE CONCRETE, his back against the wheel of a
police car. Spattered with blood. His hands, his face, his overcoat.
He mustn't be alarmed: it's not his blood. The kid lies a few meters
away, dead, in a red puddle. The porn shop window destroyed by
the impact. The sex dolls and artifacts knocked over. The pink
lights of the establishment intensify the color of the blood coming
from the corpse and flowing down the sidewalk toward a sewer.

A plainclothes policeman helps him stand. It's hard for him to
keep his balance. The clerk thinks he needs to show him his papers,
to identify himself. Get lost, the policeman orders. Nothing happened here. Nobody saw anything. We all have a bad night sometimes. By tomorrow he'll forget. Forgetting is healthy. You can't live
in your memory all the time, he tells him. The clerk asks what crime
the kid committed. None of your business, the cop says. Go home,
he says. The cop seems like a good guy. You can't judge people by
their jobs. Surely he must have a family, a wife, children. Surely they
love, respect, and admire him. Therefore, when he returns home
after a day's work, the policeman finds love.

Kill or die, he thinks he heard the dead boy say. Brave kid. His
own motto, on the other hand, is submit and survive. He thinks
about El Viejito. He compares the dead boy with El Viejito. El Viejito is so like him. Tiny, fragile since birth, weeks in an incubator,
he showed a remarkable resistance to suffering. And in spite of all
those weeks when every second seemed to be his last, he survived.
El Viejito will never be like that boy who's just been shot to death.
And neither will he. Cowards, both of them, he thinks.

But soon he convinces himself that it isn't true. In his case, it's
not a question of submitting and surviving. If he's kept going for
so long, it wasn't because of cowardice, but rather hope, a longing
for a transcendent experience: love. Because love, he knew, would
eventually bring him a new perspective on life. He's in love. Love

cures you of all servility. Love is the energy that re-orients him even as he staggers, steering him back toward the subway entrance. Love makes you see things differently, he thinks. No way is this an attack of sudden dementia. This is love. Love, he repeats to himself. Love.

As he says it, in a soft voice, he feels like he's whispering *love* to the secretary.

He walks away. The farther he goes, the less bloody his footprints become.

48

He walks in the night. Plunging into the fog, he reasons that God, if he exists, has to remember him. He doesn't deserve the life he's living. Unless God is testing him. Hope is the last thing you lose. And now he hopes for a miracle. A miracle to save his soul, but also one that will straighten out his life.

A burning cross appears on his path. The cross, its brilliance. A temple. He can hear the organ, a choir. Children's and women's voices. *Quando corpus morietur.* He walks toward the music. In the pauses of the canticle, the invocations of a hoarse voice with a Brazilian accent. The sermon has its rhythm. *Irmaos,* exclaims a thunderous voice. *Cómo castiga Deus nuestros pecadus?* it asks. How does God punish our sins? *Deus,* it pronounces, *pecadus.* The pastor answers his own question: By excluding us. When we sin, God excludes us from love. Divine love is not the same as desire. Desire is always egotistical and carnal. Desire is the root of all evil, he proclaims. The pastor offers an example: Before it punishes relations with one's neighbor's wife, the Heavenly Book punishes desire. Desire for power, desire for fame, desire for revenge. All desire will be punished. But if one repents, the Lord will grant him forgiveness:

Test me, O Lord, and try me. Examine my heart and my mind.

The pastor says that he was born in the jungle, where the Evil One lurks hidden like a savage beast. Faith kept him away from vice. Faith kept him from drink and drugs. Faith kept him from gambling and sex. Faith brought him a new life when he entered the temple of light. If we all look toward heaven, he says, and we look to the heights, heaven will open. If we repent, heaven will open. If we all confess, heaven will open. If we all join our hands in prayer, heaven will open. If we all pray, heaven will open, spilling divine light upon the earth.

Faith, shouts the pastor. And the flock repeats: Faith. A wind of voices envelops the clerk.

Anointed, he enters the temple. The pastor opens his arms to him:

I am worn out with my groaning. All night long I flood my bed with weeping and drench my couch with tears. My eyes grow weak with sorrow.

The worshippers withdraw, astonished. They notice his bloodstains. But the blood seems to stimulate the pastor's evangelical fervor. Approach the pulpit, he invites him. Confess his sins before his brothers and sisters and repent, just as all those present have done.

The origin of guilt is divine. What would become of us without guilt, he asks. And he replies: Nothing. To be on earth is to be guilty. Or nothing. Between guilt and nothingness, we, God's creation, choose guilt.

The pastor makes his way among the men, women, and children who sing and pray. In spite of the marks etched on their faces by pain, in spite of the simplicity of their clothing, these men, women, and children have been made invulnerable by faith. He now feels like one more parishioner. Now he really is starting to feel like someone else, the Other. And he likes this Other whom he is starting to be. Goodness purifies him. A complete spiritual renewal, as the pastor says, his Brazilian pronunciation turning the "s" of *spiritual* into *esh* and the "t" into *ch*, *Eshpirichual*. The pastor's eyes penetrate him like an X-ray.

Here among the brothers and sisters are those who used to beat their wives and children, those who cross-dressed to satisfy their sexual urges, those who lost everything to cocaine, those who stole from their aged mothers. The pastor names a sin. And one of the faithful cries out, asking forgiveness. The pastor approaches the sinner. The sinner kneels. The pastor blesses him. Then he names another sin, another of the faithful leaps up, and he blesses him, too.

If the word of heaven didn't have this divine force, a new brother wouldn't arrive at the temple every night.

The pastor is referring to him; he's the new brother, and just as divine force brought him to the temple, so too will the heavenly word illuminate him. The pastor cites Jonah. In the belly of the whale, Jonah prayed to God:

You hurled me into the depths, into the very heart of the seas,
and the currents swirled about me;
all your waves and breakers swept over me.
I said, "I have been banished from your sight;
yet I will look again toward your holy temple."
The engulfing waters threatened me,
the deep surrounded me;
seaweed was wrapped around my head.
When my life was ebbing away,
I remembered you, Lord,
and my prayer rose to you,
to your holy temple.
And the Lord commanded the fish, and it vomited Jonah
onto dry land.

Because the heavenly word was written to be uttered, the pastor explains. And once uttered, he will become the Other. And the Other, by reciting his sins, will save his soul from the fires of the Evil One. The pastor receives him with open arms. The organ makes the temple quake. As he embraces him, the pastor grabs him by the back of the neck, forcing him to kneel. His hand is a pincer. Those claws don't match the pastor's saccharine expression. We were all waiting for a miracle tonight, the pastor says. And the miracle came. The miracle is our new brother. We must welcome our new brother, a penitent brother whom God has sent to us as proof of his existence. Behold the miracle. We can feel heaven's energy throughout the temple, he says, spreading his arms wide to encompass the men, women, and children who now hum a gentle melody, like a murmur.

He, the new brother, must be ashamed of his past, the pastor advises. And he drags him to the pulpit. There is a basin of water. He must wash away his impurities, the pastor says. The clerk washes his hands. But that's not enough for the pastor. He grabs him by the back of the neck and submerges his head in the water. He has to get rid of it all, the pastor shouts. He must surrender to penitence and confess his vileness, his despicable acts, his weaknesses, his wretchedness. He must list them, one by one, before his sisters and brothers, he says. And he plunges his head into the basin again and again. His brothers and sisters were also swine in the earthly pigsty, and now, thanks to the luminous force of heaven, they are reborn into divine energy. He mustn't be afraid, says the pastor, leaning over him. Once more the clerk feels the pincers on the back of his neck. Let him repent and confess, the pastor drones on. The pastor is so close to him that he can smell his breath, a warm, fruity breeze.

He trembles. The pastor shakes him. Along with the shaking he thinks he can feel convulsions. If he wants to be a reborn brother, he mustn't fear repentance, but rather punishment from heaven, a punishment more awful than the punishment doled out by human beings. Because God is merciless. *Confiesi*, he orders. The voice bellows in his ears. Weeping, he hides his face in his hands, and spasms contract his stomach. His tears, the pastor believes, are a sign of redemption. Repent and *confiesi*, he demands, squeezing his neck. The pressure forces him to his knees, but he frees himself. There is now a palpable silence in the temple. The pastor looks at him. Everyone looks at him. Slowly, he stands. The pastor looks at him and waits. Everyone looks at him and waits. The pastor's eyes are red. The eyes of the faithful are red. Their mouths are maws. Their teeth grind. He starts to run. Behind him, the pastor's voice calls him a renegade. The faithful try to stop him. They tug on his overcoat. But he doesn't stop.

He runs. He runs and disappears once again into the fog.

49

THE LAST SUBWAY ARRIVES EMPTY. In the last seat of the last car, he grumbles to himself. Broken words. He repeats that gesture, the one that looks like he's shooing a fly. He removes his overcoat, his jacket; he loosens his tie. On all fours, with his limp, he walks like an injured dog. He walks up and down the subway car, howling. Like a cloned dog. At last, he tells himself, he doesn't have to explain his actions to anyone. He's afraid this might be another dream. But it's too real. His head knocks against the window.

He doesn't know if what's happening to him now is happening yesterday or tomorrow. Now becomes hazy. It's today, but it's also tomorrow. What's even worse: this train trip is happening the day after tomorrow.

When the doors open, he blinks. He hurries to get off the train. He looks at his hands. They're dirty. If they're dirty, he observes, it's because he'd been walking on all fours. It wasn't a dream. Confused, he wipes his palms on his overcoat. The escalator.

He enters the building, ignoring the elevator and taking the stairs. On all fours, he climbs up. But at the door of the apartment he needs to return to a human condition. Panting, he stands, hunts for the keys. Once inside, in the shadows, he undresses. His human condition has remained behind: he is a dog. He's tempted to bark, but he holds back. He still hasn't been sufficiently animalized, he says to himself. As he walks around the apartment, naked and on all fours, his perception of the place changes. A dog, he thinks, is guided by instinct. And what could better represent instinct in his new condition than the sense of smell? He's a dog, a dog lurking on all fours, exploring the dwelling inch by inch. Even though he's used to the filth generated by the woman and the litter, he never imagined how much dirt could accumulate on the floor, in the corners. Breadcrumbs, cigarette butts, pits, candy wrappers, corks, lint, teabags, hair curlers, peels, chewing gum, a tampon. Even a few chicken bones. Garbage. Wherever his snout sniffs, he finds filth.

Still sniffing, he enters the darkness of the litter's room. Here the stench grows thicker, condensing the odor of shoes with the grime of clothing. The radiator heats all of it into a single smell. The litter sleeps, immersed in fumes. This stink, he calculates, came from him. It's the smell of his being, he says to himself.

A light goes on. What is he doing, his wife inquires. What is he doing naked and on his hands and knees at this time of the morning. If he'd like, she'll put a dog collar and muzzle on him. She'll feed him from a tin bowl. If he'd like, she'll walk him down the street so he can pee on the trees, she says. But her humor doesn't last long. Better not try acting crazy in order to miss work, she says. He can't fool her, she goes on. If his idea is to be committed to a madhouse, she assures him, before they shove him into a straitjacket, she'll give him such a beating, he won't need electroshock to get his wits back.

50

THE CLERK DREAMS THAT HE FALLS ASLEEP on his last train ride and dreams that he's a dog. The dog falls asleep. And when he wakes, he's the last clerk to fall asleep on the last subway train. When he wakes, the reality is more terrible than before the dream. Because when he wakes, he's a man again. Tonight, when he wakes up at the back of the last car of the last subway, he has the feeling his destiny is written. He wonders which is harder, waking someone who's asleep, or someone who, awake like him, dreams that he's awake.

Also tonight: the cold, the acid rain. And also tonight, every so often, the helicopters' searchlights pierce the darkness. A shadow among shadows, he returns home. His wife and the litter are asleep. He opens the gas valve. The hiss of gas spreading through the apartment. To close the file once and for all. It makes him smile to associate what he's doing with a bureaucratic situation.

With his last glance at the apartment comes a strange melancholy. How can it be that detaching himself from suffering brings him sorrow. No doubt the sorrow comes from what he feels for El Viejito. But, he reflects, this is the best thing he can do for him. He'd like to feel happier, not sadder, but it's hard for him. Now that he's the Other at last, he feels sorry for the one he was a moment ago. Closing the door and walking down to the street, the one carrying out these actions is the Other.

He wanders into the night. It seems to him he isn't limping too badly. His footsteps are agile. He feels light. As he passes a shop window, he looks at his reflection. He doesn't look like a guy who's just exterminated his family. No doubt those who maintain that the face is a reflection of the soul are mistaken. A murderer can have a kind face, the expression of a sacristan, a pleasant demeanor. All his life he's been a fearful individual who tried to go unnoticed. And now, even now when he's the Other, his features and his smile are still the same. He practices different smiles before the shop window. From a smile that strikes him as saintly to another one he thinks looks perverse. He wonders which will be his real smile from now on.

Fatigue, more mental than physical. It startles him to have dreamed of the killing in such realistic detail. And yet, the realism of the dream made him realize that multiple crimes aren't necessary to carry out the most important part of his plan. Now he'll tell the young woman all about it.

51

TV BLOOD DOESN'T SPLATTER. Not physically, anyway. It's a moral splattering. But since conscience can be impenetrable, seeing that blood might not affect you. The same thing happens with fire. An explosion, flames. But the fire doesn't spread: it's a non-thermal sensation. Unless you're sensitive enough be stirred up by those images. But no one is that sensitive. If TV images can give you a fever, it's because you're addicted to TV, hours and hours in front of the screen.

Then, passing by a home goods store, with TV sets in the window, the clerk sees that service station just as it explodes and flies through the air. An intense black cloud with a fiery core. Gas pumps, cars, the mini-mart, the 24-hour bar, men, women, fragments of plastic, metal, and pieces of flesh enveloped in the glow of the fire.

A caption on the screen announces that these are exclusive images, that the young service station employee had announced what she was about to do and recorded herself on a cell phone, speaking to the camera. She moves her lips calmly. Her voice is inaudible through the window glass, but it must be as subtle as her lips.

He recognizes the girl whose image is reproduced on all the screens. It's the little redhead. That girl, multiplied, and all the other, identical girls, are talking directly to him.

52

HE'LL TALK TO HER. He'll tell her once more that it doesn't matter if the creature coming to life in the liquid darkness of her womb isn't his. He'll reveal his plan. If he's come to find her, he'll say, it's because he always feels like a better person when he's by her side. The secretary has worked the miracle of making him feel better than what he is. If he didn't feel better than what he is when he's with her, he wouldn't have drawn up an infallible plan.

The kiosk is on the next street, a yellow light that blinks at the base of the apartment block. As he draws closer, the volume of the cumbia increases. He can see the boys and girls dancing, drunk. He's no longer afraid to walk past the kiosk, make his way through the mob.

He walks determinedly, ready for combat. He would love it if the girl could see him, fists tight, chest out, firm steps. A gladiator, he says to himself. From the crowd: Belching. Swearing. The gladiator challenges the laughter blending with the cumbia. He's pushing through the mob, but nobody notices him. He slows his pace, his eyes inflamed by nerve. He bumps into a girl who's dancing by herself, but she doesn't even see him.

The fact that the gang ignores him is startling. If he doesn't exist for others, his nerve doesn't exist, either. If his nerve doesn't exist, he deduces, what he's experiencing is another one of his dreams. It torments him to think that tonight might be another illusion. As he stops in front of the building, he looks up, hoping to see a light in her window.

He buzzes the intercom: two short pulses. There's no answer. He waits. He bites the cuticle of his left index finger. Again, a longer pulse. He wonders how much time has passed between the two short pulses and the long one. He paces in a circle. He counts three minutes by the clock. He buzzes again: one, two, three, and a longer one. He counts five minutes. Five eternal minutes. He wonders whether she's home or not. And if she is, why she isn't responding. She might be with another guy. He thinks about the boss. She's pregnant by the boss, he says to himself. Six minutes. She's pregnant by the boss, and he's convincing her to have an abortion. The waiting is unbearable. Eight minutes. Maybe she's already had the abortion. Which would explain the wall she's built between them.

Get over your anxiety, he concentrates. Clear away all negative thoughts. If he has the nerve to disturb the young woman's rest at this early hour of the morning, he rationalizes, it's for a noble cause: love. Maybe love isn't a cause, he reconsiders. There's no feeling more generous, he argues. But he still has his doubts. He wonders if love might not be pure egotism, if perhaps he loves the young woman, because she, by fooling herself, makes him, in turn, believe himself to be better than he really is. This is usually why people fall in love, he thinks. A person falls in love because his beloved makes him feel better than he is. In love, the Other doesn't matter. What matters is how the Other makes us feel. Without the Other, we're nothing.

After this internal debate, he says to himself, he shouldn't buzz the intercom again. He should go away instead of buzzing.

But he rings again.

53

A YOUNG GUY WALKS DOWN THE HALL toward the main entrance of the building and opens the door, ready to leave. When the guy sees the clerk, he hesitates. The guy has uncombed hair, dark circles under his eyes, the shadow of a beard; his is a gypsy kind of beauty. The disarray he reflects suggests that he's coming from a restless night. The clerk wonders if the guy might have just been with her. After all, he says to himself, he knows very little about her. His distrust comes to the fore, obliging him to suspiciously measure this man who, in turn, mistrusts him. As he opens the door, the guy studies him, too, and looks at him fiercely, without letting him in, until the clerk tells him which floor he's going to, which apartment.

The elevator ride is slow. Like the first night he came to this building, as he enters the corridor, he thinks that there's something funereal about this sleeping lineup of beehives. A tomb. Behind each one of the doors facing the hallway, dead lives. The echo of his footsteps. He should turn around and leave while there's still time, he thinks. Don't be a coward, the Other goads him. Kick that whore's door down. But he objects: better to leave now, before his nerves ruin everything. But it's too late. The doorbell. A cicada at dawn.

He opens his overcoat, adjusts his tie, smooths his jacket, trying to improve his image. A nearly undetectable movement at the peephole. He smiles. Waits. The hoarse, indifferent voice asks him what he wants at this ungodly hour, what was he thinking, who does he think he is.

She opens the door a crack. She blinks. Her hair is disheveled, her lipstick smeared. His desire is rekindled. Would she please let him in, it's urgent, he needs to tell her something. Have pity on him, he begs. He's not worried about humiliating himself. It won't take him more than a moment. She opens the deadbolt and lets him in. Just a few minutes, she warns him. He nods.

The room in half-darkness. The young woman sits in one chair and he in another. They face each other. He hesitates before speaking. He looks around. The painted dishes on the walls, the figurines, the doilies and tablecloths beneath the vases with artificial flowers, the abundance of teddy bears, the carpet with a vaguely oriental pattern. Also: framed diplomas, one for teaching English, one in Accounting. A picture of her as a little girl, in a white First Communion dress, the mother-of-pearl reliquary, the hands folded in prayer. Suddenly he notices that there are two glasses with traces of brandy on the coffee table.

He remembers the guy who just came out of the building when he tried to enter. Why not suspect that guy of being with her. He wonders if it would be acceptable to question the young woman at this point. Who is she, he wants to know. Whose baby is that. Why deny that she might be leading another, secret life of vice. The word *vice*, he says to himself, is appropriate if he takes into account the appearance of that guy coming out of the building. Who was that guy. He tells himself she never was the little saint in the First Communion photo. Didn't she, after all, on successive romantic encounters, reveal her sick penchant for sexual exploration? He bites his lower lip: he asks nothing. A single question would sound like a jealous rage. The attitude he must take is one of supplicant. After all, two glasses of brandy don't mean that much.

The young woman looks at her reflection in both glasses, and, forestalling any commentary, asks him not to meddle in her life. He hasn't come here to argue. He's come to save her, he says. Then he corrects himself: they'll both be saved, he says. Also the infant she's carrying in her womb. She replies that she doesn't need anyone to save her from anything. That she can take care of herself very well. That she's been able to get along by herself till now, and that she'll continue to do so. Alone. He's about to reply that she didn't do such a great job of it, considering her affair with the boss. But he bites his lower lip, he holds back. He's come with an open heart, he says. Tomorrow, he says, or rather today, today, because at this time of morning it's already today, something extraordinary is going to happen at the office. An extraordinary occurrence that will change their lives. She remains silent. He persists: she has to believe in him. Please listen to him. If he didn't love her, he says, he wouldn't have come over at this hour, before the extraordinary event, to tell her what he's got planned. Pay attention to him, he says. With his hands in his overcoat pockets, he feels like the hero of a noir film. He walks around the coffee table and the chairs while he explains his plan: embezzlement, escape, beach, daiquiris, palm trees. The boss has always treated him like a lackey. But he's no lackey and certainly no loser behind a desk, he emphasizes. And he winks at her. In great detail, he describes how he will carry out his plan. His plan can't fail, he says. He smiles a winner's smile. He asks her if she wants to act in his film. She'll be the star. He swears she will.

The young woman looks at him. She looks at him silently. Expectations eat him alive. She'll never in her life have another opportunity likes this, he says. He doesn't understand why she's staring at him so distantly. He can't be dreaming this situation, too.

If she's still unsure of her feelings for him, he says, she shouldn't worry. In time she'll learn to love him, he says. Besides, with the fortune they're going to have, she won't lack for anything. The plan is perfect, he insists. Now or never, he says. Crying, he begs her. Please, he sobs. Now or never.

Behind him, a hand rests on his shoulder.

54

DOES HE WANT TO ADD ANYTHING ELSE, the boss asks. He's in an undershirt and is zipping up his pants. So, in a few hours an extraordinary event will take place at the office, he repeats.

The infant in her belly isn't his, she tells him. It's the boss's. What was he thinking, the boss says. The extraordinary event here, the boss says, is that he's going to be a father. And not a father of little Balkan babies, either. He's going to be the father of his own children. Twins. We'll send them to private school, she says. They're learn kickboxing.

The boss orders him to get out. He pushes him out of the apartment, pushes him down the hallway, pushes him down the stairs. He bumps himself on every step: his back, his head, his legs. He twists an arm. He rolls down the hall on the ground floor. His forehead is bleeding. The boss opens the door.

And, limping, the clerk plunges into the night.

55

Dawn, the fog of dawn. Somewhere, a bomb. Then sirens. Another day in the city. Two drug dealers on a motorcycle gun down a minister. At almost the same time, at a school, two boys and a girl load a bazooka and liquidate teachers and students. Two helicopters have to intervene to eliminate the shooters. Going after terrorists, the army surrounds a slum. After prolonged combat, they arrest hundreds of people. Then the soldiers sprinkle the settlement with napalm. An explosive device on the subway kills the passengers on an entire train and blocks a tunnel. The government announces that the war on terrorism is coming to an end; the economy is booming, and inflation is minimal, which has stimulated consumerism for the last month. Tonight there will be a new kickboxing match. And the seats are sold out. Breaking news: another fire at a nursing home. Death toll is estimated to be around fifty. The weather forecast predicts cloudiness, acid rain. Today around noon, according to astronomers, there will be a total eclipse of the sun. The moon and the sun will be positioned in the same line. Under those conditions, the whole region will be covered in darkness. The sun will disappear and it will become night. The darkness will be like that of a night with a full moon. However, nobody will pay too much attention to this phenomenon. For some time now in the city it's been hard to distinguish day from night.

For him, now is always, and it's always nighttime. He walks. He wanders the streets. He walks. Sometimes he turns around to see if the Other is following him. But no. He walks. There's no Other anymore. He's alone. He walks alone. A cloned dog comes up to him, growls, and then moves on. He doesn't even exist for the dogs. When he thinks about yesterday, he thinks about the time before yesterday, he thinks about what he hoped for when he still hoped. He doesn't hope anymore.

The clerk walks. With his hands in his overcoat pockets, he walks.

He doesn't have a ditch to die in.

Guillermo Saccomanno is the author of numerous novels and story collections, including *El buen dolor*, winner of the Premio Nacional de Literatura, and *77* and *Gesell Dome*, both of which won the Hammett Prize from the International Association of Crime Writers. He also received Seix Barral's Premio Biblioteca Breve de Novela for *El oficinista* and the Rodolfo Walsh Prize for nonfiction for *Un maestro*, as well as the Premio Democracia in 2014. Critics tend to compare his works to those of Dostoevsky, Tolstoy, and Faulkner.

A ndrea G. Labinger has published numerous translations of Latin American fiction. She has been a finalist three times in the PEN USA competition. Her translation of Liliana Heker's *The End of the Story* (Biblioasis, 2012) was included in *World Literature Today*'s list of the "75 Notable Translations of the Year." *Gesell Dome,* Labinger's translation of Guillermo Saccomanno's *Cámara Gesell* (Open Letter Books, 2016), won a PEN/Heim Translation Award.

**OPEN
LETTER**

WWW.OPENLETTERBOOKS.ORG

OPEN LETTER

WWW.OPENLETTERBOOKS.ORG